So Dead the Rose

KENDELL FOSTER CROSSEN
Writing as
M.E. CHABER

STEEGER BOOKS / **2020**

PUBLISHED BY STEEGER BOOKS
Visit steegerbooks.com for more books like this.

PUBLISHING HISTORY

Hardcover
New York: Rinehart & Co., February 1959.
Toronto: Clarke, Irwin & Co., 1959.
London: T. V. Boardman (American Bloodhound Mystery #286), January 1960.

Paperback
New York: Pocket Books #1274, March 1960. Cover by Jerry Allison.
New York: Paperback Library (63-396), A Milo March Mystery, #11, August 1970. Cover by Robert McGinnis.

ISBN: 978-1-61827-517-2

Milo March is a hard-drinking, womanizing, wisecracking, James-Bondian character. He always comes out on top through a combination of personality, bluff, bravado, luck, skill, experience, and intellect. He is a shrewd judge of human character, a crack shot, and a deeper character than I have found in most of the other spy/thriller novels I've read. But, above all, he is a con-man—and a very good one. It is Milo March himself who makes the series worth reading.

—Don Miller, *The Mystery Nook* fanzine 12

Steeger Books is proud to reissue twenty-three vintage novels and stories by M.E. Chaber, whose Milo March Mysteries deliver mile-a-minute action and breezily readable entertainment for thriller buffs.

Milo is an Insurance Investigator who takes on the tough cases. Organized crime, grand theft, arson, suspicious disappearances, murders, and millions and millions of dollars—whatever it is, Milo is just the man for the job. Or even the only man for it.

During World War II, Milo was assigned to the OSS and later the CIA. Now in the Army Reserves, with the rank of Major, he is recalled for special jobs behind the Iron Curtain. As an agent, he chops necks, trusses men like chickens to steal their uniforms, shoots point blank at secret police—yet shows compassion to an agent from the other side.

Whatever Milo does, he knows how to do it right. When the work is completed, he returns to his favorite things: women, booze, and good food, more or less in that order....

THE MILO MARCH MYSTERIES

Hangman's Harvest

No Grave for March

The Man Inside

As Old as Cain

The Splintered Man

A Lonely Walk

The Gallows Garden

A Hearse of Another Color

So Dead the Rose

Jade for a Lady

Softly in the Night

Uneasy Lies the Dead

Six Who Ran

Wanted: Dead Men

The Day It Rained Diamonds

A Man in the Middle

Wild Midnight Falls

The Flaming Man

Green Grow the Graves

The Bonded Dead

Born to Be Hanged

Death to the Brides

The Twisted Trap: Six Milo March Stories

For Lisa

She was a phantom of delight
When she gleamed upon my sight ...
—William Wordsworth

CONTENTS

9 / *So Dead the Rose*

231 / *About the Author*

ONE

Up to a point it was like any other morning in the week. I reached my office on Madison Avenue at about ten o'clock. The floor was covered with letters that the postman had shoved through the door. I scooped them up and went to my desk. I lit a cigarette and started opening the mail. It was usual, too—up to a point. The phone company wanted money. My subscription to Celebrity Service was about to expire. Someone wanted me to contribute to a charity fund. A restaurant wanted me to pay my bill—a big bill, which had been run up there mostly because the bartender made his dry martinis with Beefeater gin. Somebody else wanted me to subscribe to a magazine. And then there was a letter that started off in a very friendly fashion with "Greetings." I'd almost finished reading it before I realized it was informing me that I had just been recalled to active duty with the United States Army.

When I finished cursing, I read it again, hoping there was a mistake. But there wasn't. It said very clearly that Major Milo March of the Army Reserve was recalled to active duty. That was certainly me. Normally it's Milo March, insurance investigator. Which means that if you bump off your favorite uncle because he's loaded with the green stuff, and the cops don't get you right away, I'm sent out to look for you. But then

I'd also made the mistake of getting caught in a little donny-brook known as World War II, serving in the OSS, and since then I'd been called back to active duty twice.* Each time it had meant nothing but trouble for me, and this time would probably be no different.

I calmed down a little more and took another look at the letter. I was supposed to report in Washington. The time was twenty-one hundred. Or nine o'clock at night. The date was the same date as the morning I was reading the letter. The place was a room number in a Washington hotel.

That made me curse even more, for I knew what it meant. There was only one man in the entire army who would think of having me report for active duty at nine o'clock at night in a Washington hotel room. But there wasn't much I could do about it and there wasn't even too much time to brood about it.

I was busy the rest of the day. Fortunately, I didn't have any cases that were active at the moment, but there were a couple of small local cases that would have to be worked on soon. I arranged for Eddie Coady, another investigator, to take them over. I checked in everything else with my attorney and gave my answering service instructions where to route which calls. I paid up the outstanding bills. Then I went down to the Village to my apartment and dug out an old uniform. It still fit and it was reasonably clean, so I took it around the corner and had it pressed.

By the time I was packed and tricked out like the Army's

---

* See *No Grave for March* and *The Splintered Man* by M.E. Chaber. (All footnotes were added by the editor.)

idea of the well-dressed man, it was only about two hours before I had to catch the plane for Washington. I took my suitcase and walked over to the Blue Mill on Commerce Street. Alcino, behind the bar, gave me a mock salute and wanted to know if it was Boy Scout week. I gave him a rude answer, in Portuguese so that I wouldn't shock the nice old ladies who were sitting next to me and sipping their manhattans. After that I ordered a martini. I repeated the order a couple of times and then went into the back and had a steak dinner. By the time I'd finished I had to leave for LaGuardia Airport.

It was just about eight o'clock when I landed in Washington. That still gave me a little time, so I went into a bar and had a triple order of Seagram's VO. It made me feel more military.

I took a taxi to the hotel. Since I wasn't sure about the next step, I checked my bag and then I went up to the room number I'd been given in the letter. I knocked on the door.

"Come in," a voice called.

I opened the door and stepped inside. The room was extremely dark. Before I could react to that, someone pushed the door shut behind me. That completed the darkness.

Something pressed against my side. It felt suspiciously like a gun. *"Kto idyot?"* a voice asked. The language was Russian.

"Moya familiya March," I said, automatically answering in the same language. *"Ya by khotyel posmotryet vasha komandir."*

"Gde vy zhiveot—" he started to say.

That's when I went into action. He'd talked enough so that I had a good mental picture of him. I swung quickly away from the pressure against my back, pivoting on one foot and launching one fist in the direction the voice had come from. My knuckles connected solidly with flesh, the impact jarring pleasantly along the muscles of my arm. There was a crash as the victim bounced off the wall and hit the floor.

"All right," I said tightly. "Somebody had better turn on some lights. And if General Roberts is in the room, he'd better start hiding behind those stars."

There was a click and a light went on. I'd been right. There were four other men in the room. Two of them were civilians whom I'd seen before. One was George Hillyer, the head of Central Intelligence Agency, and the other was Philip Emerson, his assistant. The third man wore an army uniform with three stars on each shoulder. His name was Sam Roberts and it seemed to me that every time I saw him he'd just gotten a new promotion. The fourth man was sitting on the floor, rubbing his chin and trying to get the dazed expression off his face. He wore the uniform of a captain in the Army. I'd never seen him before.

"Old slippery Sam," I said to General Roberts. I figured I had a right to talk that way to him. In World War II, I'd worked behind the lines with him when he was only a chicken colonel. Every time I'd seen him since then it had meant trouble for me. "I figured you were in this somewhere. Nobody else would think of making a man report for active duty at nine o'clock at night at a hotel room. And there isn't another idiot in the service who would have the reporting man walk into a dark room."

The two civilians were concealing grins, but General Roberts ignored me. He was looking at the Captain on the floor. "Well, Captain," he said, "how was his Russian?"

"Very good, sir," the Captain said. He grinned ruefully. "So are, I might add, his reflexes and his right."

"Sorry I hit you, Captain," I said, "but it's one of the risks of serving under a commanding officer who insists on indulging in childish games."

"Silence," roared the General. He was glaring at me, his face darkly red. "Major March, you are the most insubordinate, disrespectful, disobedient officer I ever had the misfortune to command. For two cents I'd break you to a second lieutenant and send you to Alaska."

"Yes?" I said. "Who's going to pull your chestnuts out of the fire if you do that?"

The two civilians were now grinning openly. General Roberts was struggling manfully with his temper. "What do you mean by that?" he demanded.

"You know damn well what I mean," I said. "This is the third time you've called me back to active duty. The first two times it was to do something you didn't think your regular boys could do. Why should I think this is any different—especially after that jazz you pulled on me as I came in?"

One of the civilians decided to help the General get off the hook. It was Hillyer. "After all, General," he said pleasantly, "I think we agreed when we used Major March before that his attitude was somewhat unusual, at least in military circles, but that the results made it worthwhile. As a matter of fact, it was you yourself who first convinced us of this. And we all agreed that he was the man for the present assignment before he was recalled to active duty."

"I suppose so," General Roberts said slowly. Some of the color had faded from his face. He stared at me. "Under the circumstances, Major March, we'll forget that we're both in uniform. But I sometimes wonder why I didn't have you summarily shot when we were both overseas during the war."

"That's easy," I said. "We were all alone behind enemy lines and you couldn't have found a firing squad. Besides, if you could have had me shot, there wouldn't have been anybody to bring you out."

He started to darken up again.

"Anyway," Hillyer said quickly, "we're all glad to have you back working with us again, Major March."

"Well, I can't say the same thing," I said. "I'm getting tired of being dragged away from my business every time you characters stub your toes." I looked at the General and grinned. "You must've been a busy little bee since I saw you last. You've got an extra star on each shoulder. That's a big jump from those chicken wings you used to wear."

He started to turn purple, but then suddenly it was over. He relaxed and gave me the nearest thing to a grin he could manage. "Damnit, Milo," he said, "someday you're going to go too far."

"You've been saying that for as long as I've known you," I said. "Remember the night we were in France to blow up a bridge and the Marquis was supposed to send us two helpers? The two turned out to be girls. That's what you said to me then because I took the prettiest one."

There was nothing like the mention of a war to jolly up the General. He actually managed a full-scale smile this time. "That was quite a night," he said. Then he realized that the Captain was standing there with his mouth hanging open, and he wiped the smile from his face, clearing his throat loudly. "It was quite a war, Milo, my boy." Only a general would describe a war as quite a war. "Well, this isn't getting to our problem."

"You got a better one?" I asked, winking at the Captain.

The General ignored it. "We have a rather serious problem," he said. "Not very big, but still serious."

"Just a minute," I said. "Am I recalled to active duty for just this one job, or are you going to try to make a permanent thing out of it?"

"Just for this one job, Major," Hillyer said. "As soon as it's finished you can go back to your civilian job."

"That's right," General Roberts said, in a tone of voice that said he didn't understand why anyone would want to be a civilian. "It shouldn't take you more than three or four days and then you're through. You have my word for that."

"Your word," I said scornfully. "From that trick at the door, it would seem that you're interested in how well I've retained my Russian. That hardly sounds like a three- or four-day job."

"It's not in Russia," the General said quickly. "You may need to remember your Russian, though. Civilian life softens some men."

"I like that kind of softening," I told him. "What's the job?"

"An important paper has vanished," Hillyer said. "From our Paris office. If it is not recovered, hundreds of people will die."

"It must be a pretty important paper," I said.

"It is. It contains a complete list of our contacts behind the Iron Curtain. In code, of course, but it will be only a matter of time before they manage to break the code. It must be recovered before they do."

"What about your men over there?" I asked. "You must have plenty of them available."

"We do," Hillyer said, "but we have reason to think that most of them, perhaps all, are known to members of the Russian Embassy. At the best, we will have only one try to get it back. At least before it goes to Russia. So we don't dare risk missing that one chance."

"When did it vanish?"

"Yesterday. We had a meeting the minute we learned about it, and decided you were the best man to get it back. Your recall to active duty was put through at once."

I nodded. That explained the big rush in the order to report. "I guess you'd better tell me the whole story," I said.

"There is a minor clerk in the Paris office," Hillyer said. "His name is Roger Adams. He has always been considered a good security risk. Consequently he had access to all the files. It now seems that he recently became involved with a girl in the Russian Embassy without any of our people knowing about it. As we get it, he wanted to prove to her that he was more important than he is, so he took a paper at random from the files and showed it to her. When she asked him for it, he gave it to her. Apparently he did not even know what the paper contained since he was not cleared to know the code."

"Pretty," I said. "How did you find out about it?"

"The clerk came and told us. As soon as he was away from her, he began to realize what he'd done, so he confessed the whole thing."

"Must be some girl," I said.

"That seems to be the impression he gives," Hillyer said dryly.

"Do you know who the girl is?" I asked.

"Yes and no. Her name is Zoya Aristova. Officially she is a clerk in the Russian Embassy, but she may be a member of either the MVD* or the KGB. We don't know."

"Do you have anything else on it?"

"No. The girl has not been seen since Adams turned the paper over to her."

"Do you have a plan or am I just supposed to go in and play it the way it falls?"

"A little of each. The Aristova girl was usually seen in the company of another clerk in the Embassy named Maryutka Kosygina. She has been seen since. Someone in the Paris office suggested that there might be a possibility of working through her if we used a man who could pose as either a White Russian or a former defector who wants to get back to Russia. They have a plan by which you can meet her, but after that it will be up to you."

I didn't think much of the idea, but it might be difficult to work out a better one if the time was short. "Well," I said, "we'll see how it falls. What else do you have?"

---

* Ministerstvo Vnutrennikh Del (Ministry of Internal Affairs), Soviet agency of internal security. From 1954 the responsibility for secret police matters was assumed by the KGB (Komitet Gosudarstvennoy Bezopasnosti, Committee for State Security).

"That's all. There are probably more minor details which will be given to you there. You can talk to the clerk, if you like. You'll get all the assistance you need from the Paris office, but it'll be entirely up to you. Just remember that you will not have much time." Hillyer smiled sympathetically.

"Okay. When do you want me to leave?"

"Right away," General Roberts said. "In the next room, you will find a complete outfit of civilian clothes. We think it's better if you do not show up as an Army officer. There are also additional clothes and luggage. There's everything else you'll need, including your passport. As soon as you're ready, you'll be flown to Paris in an Army plane. You will be met at the airport by someone from the CIA office in Paris. He will see that you get everything else you need."

"Do you think that's wise?" I asked.

"We're pretty certain that this man is not known to the Russians," Hillyer said. "He's probably the only one not known, but it's a job beyond his capacities. You've worked with him before, Major. In fact, he also suggested that we send you on the assignment if it were possible."

"Who?" I asked.

"Henri Flambeau. He used to work in our Berlin office and was transferred to Paris about a year ago."

I remembered him. I'd worked with him the time they'd sent me to East Berlin to bring back an important prisoner. We'd gotten along fine, so it made me feel a little better to know that he was the man I'd be contacting.

"A good man," I said. "Okay. There are only a couple of

things I want to know. Am I on my own or do I have to take orders from someone over there?"

"You're on your own," General Roberts said.

"Fine. Now, how badly do you want that paper?"

"Look at it this way," General Roberts said. "If the Russians get that paper decoded, not only will several hundred people die, but more than ten years' work will be destroyed and we'll have to start all over again from the beginning. We'll even have to devise new codes, new drops all over Europe, a whole new system for getting information from behind the Iron Curtain. We want the paper back. Anything—repeat anything—short of war that will get it back will be worth it."

TWO

Everything went off fine. The civilian clothes the Army had bought for me fit. There was a good assortment of everything and just enough to fill the bag. The plane was ready not long after we got to the airport. The Army does all right as long as they're working with schedules or statistics. Like the plane. It was built for performance rather than comfort, but I still managed to sleep most of the way to Paris.

After we came down on the Paris runway, I climbed out of the plane and went into the customs office. There wasn't anyone else there, so I was soon through. I had just entered the main terminal when I heard my name called.

"Milo! Milo, *mon vieux!*"

I looked around and saw Henri Flambeau running toward me. He was a little man, looking almost like an ex-jockey. His sharp face bore the brush marks of laughter. It had been a couple of years since we had met, and I suddenly found myself being glad to see him again.

He rushed up and embraced me. "Henri," I said, "it's good to see you." I stepped back and looked at him. I grinned and quoted, *"Il y avait un jeune homme de Provence ..."* It was the first line of the French limerick Henri and I had used once before for identification between us, and I knew he'd remember it.

"*Dont les couilles étaient vraiment immenses,*" he completed the next line with a roar of laughter. "It is so good to see you, my friend. I am glad that they were able to send you."

"I'm not so glad about that," I told him. "Do you have a hotel room for me?"

"Of course. Come, we will go to it."

We went out and found a taxi. Henri gave the driver the address and we climbed in.

"How come you're here?" I asked him. "I thought you were the Berlin expert."

"Ah, but I am also an expert on Paris," he said. "Finally, I could stand those Germans no longer. They have no souls. I, Henri Flambeau, must have people around me with souls or I cannot breathe. So I ask them to transfer me to the Paris office. Here I perform the same function I did there. I am the contact with the dark underside of the belly of the world."

"You mean anything from information to false passports?" I asked.

He nodded. "Anything you want. I am still the specialist in anything that is illegal or even frowned upon. It is an accomplishment which your CIA seems to appreciate."

"I'll bet. Although they'll probably never admit it publicly."

The cab jerked to a stop and we were in front of a small hotel. Henri paid the driver and we went in. He had made a reservation for me and we were soon in the room. It was large and comfortable.

"I thought a small hotel might be best," he explained,

"since nothing is yet certain about your method of operation. However, if you don't like it ..."

"It's fine," I said.

"Do you feel like talking," he asked, "or would you rather sleep?"

"Sleep is for peasants," I said. "Besides, I slept most of the way on the flight. There wasn't anyone to talk to except the flyboy."

He glanced at my slyly. "We could go to a place where we could get a drink—unless you've given up such bad habits."

"It's for a patriotic cause," I said. "I regret that I have but one stomach to give for my country. Lead on, little one."

"Shameless!" he exclaimed. "Here only a few minutes and already calling me names! Well, come, old man."

We went down and got another cab. This time it was an even shorter ride. When we got out, we went down a flight of stairs and entered a dimly lit room. There was a small jazz band playing. A pretty African girl, wearing a minimum of clothes, stood in front of it, singing in French. Most of the tables were filled, but at the sight of Henri a waiter hurried forth and found us a table. It was in a corner of the room and was practically the only table that wasn't crowded near others. I said I'd have a double brandy, Henri decided on the same, and the waiter rushed off.

"Who are you around here?" I asked Henri. "This looks like special service of some kind."

"It is," he said. "They believe that I am an important operator. They have several tables in here which are arranged so that one may sit and talk with a client and not worry about anyone listening to the conversation."

"Sounds like a handy arrangement," I admitted. "What's the name of this charming little dump?"

"Ma Petite."

I laughed. "Ma Petite, where the elite meet to cheat?" He smiled but kept quiet as the waiter arrived with our drinks. I tasted mine and found it much better than I had expected. I said as much.

"Part of the special service," he said. "See that couple sitting at that table over there?"

I followed the direction of his gaze and saw a small, pretty blonde girl. She was absorbed in the music, beating on the table with her fingers. The man with her was a big, burly fellow who seemed bored by the whole thing. "What about them?" I asked.

"The girl is Maryutka Kosygina."

"You mean the friend?"

He nodded. "The friend of Zoya Aristova. Both of them used to come here, but the Aristova girl hasn't been here since she got the coded paper. This is where young Adams met her, incidentally."

"This place gets more and more interesting," I said. "Just what kind of place is it?"

"A little bit of everything," he said. "It is a place where many genuine jazz enthusiasts come. They can sit all evening and listen to the music and it does not cost much. If one of them wants to smoke something stronger than regular cigarettes, no one is going to get angry at him. It is also a place where a number of the shadier characters of Paris come during their idle hours. One could arrange to buy almost anything here, from an old jazz record to murder. And it is also a place where many of the smart operators come."

"Like you?"

"Like me," he said. "The two Russian girls are both jazz lovers. They used to be here almost every night. This one has been here every night since the incident."

"Who's the big guy with her?"

Henri shrugged. "I imagine what he looks to be. Probably MVD or KGB. I understand that in the beginning, when the girls first started coming here, there was always a guard with them, but finally they came alone. This one has been with her since the incident."

"Jazz has been their only reason for coming here?"

"I think so. It would be almost impossible for anyone to do anything in here without its being known."

"You saw the other girl?"

"Oh, yes," he said. He kissed the tips of his fingers. "She was a beautiful girl. One cannot blame young Adams for becoming interested in her—only for giving her a paper from the files. Most of you Americans think you have to give a woman something to show that you are fond of her. It is so childish."

"And dangerous in this case," I said. "Was Adams a jazz fan, too?"

"Yes. That was how he became acquainted with her. I understand that both girls went up to his apartment a couple of times to listen to his record collection. Later, only the Aristova girl went to his apartment."

"Apparently she forgot her interest in jazz long enough to get interested in something else. The CIA files."

"Yes. But Adams claims that she didn't ask him to do anything like that. He did it to impress her. It was only after she'd seen the paper that she asked to keep it. Just overnight. She said it would show that he trusted her, a Russian. So he fell for it."

"The Aristova girl was a clerk in the Embassy?"

He nodded.

"And this one?"

"She is listed as a secretary."

"One thing strikes me about this," I said. "My guess is, both girls must be a lot more than clerk and secretary. If that's all they were, I don't think they'd have as much freedom as these two seem to have had."

He grinned. "I wondered how soon you'd get around to that," he said with delight. "It was also my feeling, although no one else in the office has mentioned the possibility. I have kept quiet, intending to discuss it only with you."

"What do you think?" I asked.

"I did think perhaps the MVD," he said, "but I have changed my mind. Now I think at least the Aristova girl is of the KGB, the secret police. Perhaps this one, too. They were probably here for just the sort of work she did with young Adams, only in this case she fell into a bit of luck."

I looked at him. "What made you change your mind?"

"You have your work cut out for you, my friend," he said. "The Aristova girl is no longer in Paris, and you can be sure that wherever she is, there also is the missing paper."

"Where is she?"

"*Qui sait?*" he said, shrugging. "I could make a guess. Moscow. But all I know is that she took off in a Russian plane about five hours before you arrived tonight."

"How do you know?"

"I saw her myself. We've been watching the Embassy and the airport since she got the paper and disappeared. There was always a chance, of course, that she had left before Adams confessed, but we watched. I was at the airport and saw her arrive in a big limousine, heavily escorted. But she got on the plane by herself."

The waiter arrived and we ordered more brandy. We waited until he had brought it to continue with our conversation.

"That's why you're guessing the KGB?" I asked.

"Yes. I'm sure they tried to break the code here and failed. So it had to be sent back to Russia. But if a clerk got hold of such a paper, she would certainly not be entrusted to carry it back. I doubt that they would even send her if she were only a member of MVD. But if she were important in the KGB, she might very well take it back herself."

"We'd better check it a little further," I said, "but if she's taken it to Moscow, I guess that's that. We'd better send out word for all the agents behind the Curtain to head for the hills."

"Maybe," he said, "but not necessarily."

"What do you mean?" I asked.

"They tell me there are some nice vacation spots in Russia," he said, smiling at me.

"You're out of your mind," I said. "I'm no magician.

Besides, she arrives in Moscow, turns the paper over to the KGB, or whoever, and it vanishes into the inner offices for the experts to pore over it. Even if I went to Moscow, there'd be no chance of me getting within five miles of it."

"I think you may be ordered to go after it anyway," he said.

I swore. "Where'd you get this crazy idea?" I asked.

"For one thing, *mon vieux,* I suggested it."

I glared at him.

"Wait a minute, my friend," he said. "It is important, this paper, yes?"

"Yes," I admitted.

"Well, if there is a chance to get it back, you are the one man who can pull it off. To begin with, you are one of perhaps three men we have who can speak Russian like a native. Then you have the other qualifications necessary to pull off such a job. I myself have seen you do something not too different."*

"There's a big difference between going into East Berlin and going several thousand miles inside Russia."

"Not that much. It's true that we could easily get a man into Russia. He might even be dropped in by plane. But he then has to recover the paper and get out of the country. I believe that you would have the best chance of doing that, so I suggested it. I imagine that the CIA may agree with me."

"It's crazy," I said. "An army couldn't get it back."

"If I'm right," he said, "it might be done. If I'm wrong ..." He shrugged.

"Right about what?"

"Listen," he said. "This is all theory, but you agree with

---

* See *The Splintered Man.*

me on the first part of it, and if that is correct, then the rest may be, too. Some of it comes from the fact that I know the Russian Embassy setup very well, and you may never have had a need to know that. Now, there are often MVD personnel in Russian embassies, but not necessarily. On the other hand, our old friend the KGB has members in every single embassy throughout the world. Also, as you know, every Russian counterintelligence or espionage man or woman is from the KGB. They are the nearest thing to your own CIA. But do you know how they function in a matter such as this?"

"No," I admitted.

"They have their own codes and their own means of communication, which are not known to other Russian agencies, not even the MVD. Normally, when something of importance is turned up—such as this missing paper—the object or the information is transported to Moscow through the regular channels of the KGB. It is very seldom that an agent returns to give a report and carry something. The only times I have known this to be done were when the agent was someone very important who reported only to General Serov himself. This is why I think that Zoya Aristova is an important Russian spy. So important that she has carried the paper directly to Ivan Alexandrovich Serov in Moscow."

"Even if you're right," I said, "I don't see where it helps. If anything, it makes it worse. Even if I were flown to Moscow this minute, she would have already turned it over to Serov. And how the hell is anybody going to get a sheet of paper away from him?"

"Ah," he said. *"Aide-toi, le ciel t'aidera*—Heaven helps those who help themselves. But perhaps we have a little luck, too. The Russians just now are putting on a big trade show in East Berlin. It is a preview before they have an even bigger trade convention in Moscow. Security is most important there, and we have reports that General Serov himself is there in charge of the security arrangements. Khrushchev will be one of the speakers the last day. It will be another three days before Serov returns to Moscow. So the Aristova girl will have to wait at least three days to report to Serov."

"If you're right," I said.

"If I'm right," he admitted. "But I think I am."

"Only a crazy Frenchman could think of the whole thing," I said. I was irritated and it showed in my voice. I felt that way because I knew I was getting interested in his idea. That's the first step to getting hooked, and nobody knew it better than I did. "Even so, Henri, how the hell do I get into Russia? Write to Khrushchev?"

"It is formidable," Henri said. "I do not have a solution, I confess. The only thing which has occurred to me is that you might possibly enter East Berlin while the trade meeting is going on and find a way of attaching yourself to a trade delegation going back to Moscow for the meeting there."

"No," I said. "I'm sure they count noses very carefully, and an extra one would be quickly noted." I stared at him with interest. "But maybe you're closer to an idea than you know. Where are these trade delegations from?"

"All the satellites and from every part of Russia."

"Then there might be a chance," I said thoughtfully. I was

hooked, all right. "But that would put me in Moscow at the same time that Serov arrives, which wouldn't do much good."

"You might get more of an edge than that," he said. "Serov won't leave until every delegate and party representative is out of Berlin. With a little luck you might get to Moscow several hours before he does."

"And how do I find out where the girl and the paper are?"

"That way," he said, nodding in the direction of the blonde.

"That's all?" I asked with sarcasm. "If you're right, she's probably part of the KGB, too. So all I do is go up and tell her I've got a yen for her friend and what's her phone number?"

"Why not?" he said with a grin. "My friend Milo March should have no trouble getting information from a woman."

"Shut up and let me think," I said. "In the meantime, you might ply me with more liquor. If I'm going to be stupid enough to fall for all of this, I might as well have the excuse of being drunk."

He grinned and signaled for the waiter, who soon brought us two more double brandies. I sipped my drink and studied the blonde girl. She was obviously lost in the rhythms of the music. The man with her was just as obviously not. He kept looking at his watch and frowning.

"Within ten minutes," Henri said softly, "I could have him taken care of so that you could become acquainted with her."

"How?" I demanded. "Over a hot jazz record? If she's KGB, she's too smart for that. She may even be if she's nothing but a secretary. It'll take more than that, my friend."

"You will think of something, *mon vieux*," he said calmly.

"Thanks for nothing," I said dryly. "Do you think she knows you?"

"No more that she knows other regulars here."

"Are you," I asked, "also an expert on the KGB?"

"No," he said, "but we have a man here in Paris who is."

"What time is it?"

"Two-thirty."

"Can we see him tonight? There is not much time."

"I'll see," Henri said. He got up and left the table. He was back in about fifteen minutes.

"We can see him," he said. "I made two phone calls while I was at it."

"So?"

"There's been an answer from Washington. Decoded, it reads: 'March's orders are to proceed as he thinks best but lost item must be recovered at all cost.' It's signed by General Roberts."

I relieved myself of a few direct opinions about the General, but I knew it didn't make any difference. I was hooked anyway. Even if he'd said not to go, I would probably have figured a way to get around it. Intelligence work is like a disease. You get to thinking, *Can I get away with this?* Then you have to go out and prove to yourself that you can.

"Go pay the bill," I told Henri, "and wait for me outside. I'll be right with you."

"What are you going to do?"

"Make the opening move, then postpone the game until tomorrow night—I hope."

He got up and left the table without saying any more. I

watched as he found the waiter and settled the bill. Then he left the club without looking back.

I waited a few more minutes and then I got up and began to thread my way slowly among the tables. I lurched as I went as though I'd had too much to drink. I stumbled into several tables and went on without apologizing.

Finally I reached the table where the blonde sat with her burly escort. As I tried to go past them, I stumbled, jamming the table against him and knocking his drink over so that it spilled into his lap.

"Watch where you're going," he said angrily in very bad French.

I laughed at him drunkenly and winked broadly at the girl. He shoved back his chair and stood up, his face stiff with anger.

I hit him as hard as I could on the point of the jaw. The anger blanked out of his face and he fell, the chair crashing over.

"French pig," I said in Russian. *"Ostorogno, stupen!"* I turned and staggered out of the club.

THREE

The orchestra was playing loudly to cover up the incident as I left and the waiter was hurrying toward the table, but I got out quickly. Henri was not only waiting, but he had a taxi standing at the curb. He held the door open without saying anything and I stepped in. As soon as the door was closed, the taxi took off with the wild spurt that only Paris cab drivers can achieve.

"Thanks," I said.

"I have seen that look on your face before," Henri said, "so I thought there might be the need for a hurried exit. What happened?"

I gave him a fast outline of what had taken place.

"*Ça, par exemple, c'est trop fort!*" he exclaimed. "All my life I will regret that I did not stay to watch it. Did you do it for pleasure or for a purpose?"

"It'll be an opening wedge," I said, "if things work out so that I can follow it up. One thing it will do. If the girl is nothing but a secretary, she won't be back there tomorrow night. If she's a member of the KGB, then you can be sure that she will be."

"You are so right," he said delightedly. "Milo, my friend, it is such a pleasure to be working with you again. It adds to my happiness."

"If I have to do this," I said, "I'm glad that you're around—but I'd rather meet you just as a tourist. When do we get to this place we're going?"

"*Voilà*," he said as the taxi made a sudden swoop to the curb. "We are here." He paid the driver and we got out. We were standing in front of a small house somewhere in the suburbs of Paris. There was a light in one window. All the other houses on the block were dark.

"Come, *mon vieux*," Henri said. "We go. In what other branch of your government could you find a man ready to serve you at three in the morning?"

"I don't even want to find out," I muttered as I followed him up to the house.

Henri reached up and jiggled the knocker. We waited. After a couple of minutes the door opened.

"Henri?" a man's voice asked.

"*Oui*," Henri said. The door opened wider and we went inside. Once we were there, I could finally get a good look at the man who had let us in. He was a slightly stooped, scholarly-looking young man, the kind you don't expect to find in the CIA but often do.

"This is Major March," Henri said. "You two are also countrymen, so you should certainly know each other. Milo, this is William Morrison."

We shook hands. "I've heard a lot about you, Major," he said. "It's a real pleasure to meet you. Let's go in here." He led the way into a small study. There were already several bottles sitting out, as well as glasses and a bucket of ice. "Have a drink?"

"Brandy," I said.

Henri echoed me and Morrison quickly served us. Then he sat down and looked at me. "What can I do for you, Major?"

"Don't call me Major," I told him. "Those leaves get too heavy for my shoulders. I want to know a couple of things about the KGB. I suppose there is someone here in Paris who is in charge of all the agents in this area?"

"Yes," he said, nodding. "Leonid Belyayev. Outwardly, he is merely another member of Amtorg Trading Corporation here, but his real mission is to oversee all KGB operations."

"Every agent is subject to his orders?"

"Yes."

"Including those in the Embassy?"

"Especially those," he said with a smile.

"If agents from other spots," I said, "came to Paris on their way back to Moscow, would they be expected to report to him?"

"Not normally. There might be special cases."

"Would he know they were here? Or know about their assignments?"

He shook his head. "Again, not normally. He wouldn't know they existed and they wouldn't know about him, except in special cases."

"Do KGB agents have any way of recognizing each other if they meet somewhere by accident?" I asked.

"Yes," he said. "Normally, they are not supposed to fraternize, but they do have recognition signs. You have to use the words 'October' and 'Brest-Litovsk' in a sentence. The answer must contain the words 'silk gloves.' "

"All right," I said. "October for the date of the Russian Revolution, Brest-Litovsk for the place where Russia made the armistice with the German army, and the answer out of Stalin's remark that 'You cannot make a revolution with silk gloves.' "

"Right," he said with a smile. "You know a little about the subject yourself."

"Some," I admitted. "But not much about the KGB. Tell me one more thing. If the KGB agent stationed in Paris encountered another agent who was on the way through Paris, would the first agent be apt to check with Belyayev?"

"Probably not, but there is no way to be certain."

"If such a check were made, how would Belyayev react?"

"He'd probably either phone Moscow or get in touch by short wave. Belyayev is a cautious man."

I thought about it a minute. "Can you block him off for two or three hours? So that no one can get through to him on the phone?"

"Yes," he said. "That part is easy. We can have his phone out of order for that long. We might be able to keep anyone from getting to him directly, but that will be a little harder."

"No," I said. "The phone will do. If that doesn't work, nothing will help."

"What time?" he asked.

I looked at Henri. "What time should I get there tomorrow night?"

"Usually between nine and ten."

"Make it from ten to one," I told Morrison. "That should more than cover me."

"All right," he said. "I'll have to clear it through the office, but I'm sure there will be no problem. They've given top priority to your assignment."

"They'll clear it," Henri said.

"Anything else I can do?" Morrison asked.

"I don't think so," I said. "For about two hours I'm going to pretend I'm a KGB man, probably on his way from America to Moscow. Anything else I need to know?"

"Probably a million things. Is it with another KGB agent?"

"We think so."

"Then you can probably get by. Just don't give any information. Another KGB agent would expect that. From what I know, they sometimes contact each other, but they never get very chummy in terms of talking to each other about their work. So, unless you're seeing someone who is a superior, you won't need to know details."

"How would such an agent be apt to go from Paris to Moscow?"

"Unless it was something urgent, he'd go on a regular Russian flight."

"Okay," I said. "Thanks for everything. I'm sorry we had to get you up in the middle of the night."

"I'm used to it," he said with a smile. We shook hands and Henri and I left.

It was four o'clock in the morning when we got back to my hotel. I gave Henri a few things to check for me and we arranged to meet in the afternoon. I went upstairs and to sleep.

I slept until noon. I had breakfast in the hotel and then

went out to do a little shopping. I thought of calling the CIA office, but then thought better of it. They must know where I was and they could always send messages through Henri. The less I had to do with them, the better. I shopped around until I found a place with imported liquor. I bought a bottle of Seagram's VO and went back to the hotel to enjoy it.

Henri showed up at four o'clock. He bustled into my room, looking pleased with the world and himself.

"Everything goes like the house on fire," he announced. "The machinery hums and even Washington believes that the paper is as good as recovered."

"I'm glad that somebody does," I said sourly. "Now if they would only go after it."

"You will be a hero, *mon vieux*."

"I hope not," I said. "The only heroes are dead ones. Besides, I know the good General Roberts. If I bring the paper back, he will still be annoyed because I didn't bring the Politburo along with it."

"In the meantime," Henri said, shrugging, "everything you want is yours. Washington has instructed the office to give you every possible help and to provide you with unlimited funds."

"That's a lovely sound," I said. "What else?"

"I have been instructed to work with you and follow your orders. The phone of Belyayev will be out of order tonight from ten until one. Arrangements have been made to take both of us to West Germany anytime you want to leave. The plane will be standing by from ten o'clock on. Oh, incidentally there is a Russian plane leaving Paris at two in the morning bound for Moscow."

"When do we get the unlimited funds?"

"I have three hundred thousand francs with me," he said with a grin, "and we can draw whatever we need at the West Berlin office. They have also been instructed to give us complete cooperation."

"That's nice," I said. "What will they do about that big Russian I knocked out last night?"

"That is my department, my friend. If he is there tonight and is any trouble at all, you just nod to me and within ten minutes I'll have him in the hospital. Or in the Seine, if you prefer."

"Fine," I said. "Have a drink and we'll go out on the town."

We had a couple of drinks and then we left. Just because I felt like having a good martini without its being drowned in vermouth, we went first to the American bar, where we made a start on those unlimited funds. Later we went to Le Cabaret and had *blanquette de veau à l'ancienne* for dinner. With wine. We lingered over that until it was time to leave for Ma Petite. I picked up the package I had checked when we entered the restaurant and we took a cab to the club.

I let Henri enter first and I waited. When he didn't reappear within five minutes, I entered the club. As I went through the door, I scanned the room. She was sitting at the same table she had been at the night before. But this time she was alone. I hesitated in the doorway, still looking over the room. Henri was sitting where we had sat the night before. He made a slight gesture toward the back of the room with his head. A moment later I saw the reason why. The Russian who had been with the girl was now sitting alone in a far corner of the room. So the bait had been taken.

I swaggered into the room, then pretended suddenly to see the girl. I squared my shoulders and marched over to her table. I bowed. *"Izvinite,"* I said. *"A sogaleu o nedorazumenii."* I switched to very bad, halting French. *"J'en suis au regret."*

"It is all right," she said in Russian. "I understand."

"Oh, you speak my language," I said with feigned delight. "It is so good to hear it again. I have heard nothing but terrible foreign languages for years."

"Oh?" she said. "You have been away?"

"You see," I said. "All of you foreigners are alike. You act as if we were prisoners or something. The citizens of the Soviet Union have complete freedom. We can go anywhere in the world if there is a reason for going."

"Relax," she said, laughing. "I am also a Russian. I work for our Embassy here."

"Oh," I said. I looked at her with more interest. "You are alone tonight?"

"Yes."

"May I join you for a minute?"

She nodded and I sat down.

"I cannot stay long," I said. "I am leaving for home tonight."

"After being away for how long?" she asked.

"Five years," I said. "In America." I looked at her as though trying to find out what sort of person she was. "Learning how they make their machinery run."

"And now you're going back," she said. "You are lucky. When it is October—beautiful October—you'll probably be in Brest-Litovsk. That must be somewhere near your home—at least, from your accent."

"It is," I said. "It will be good to be back. Then I can take off my silk gloves and get to work."

It was as simple as that. Nothing more was said about our work, but her manner changed at once.

"The man who was with you last night," I said, "the one I hit, was he also a countryman?"

"Yes. He is with the Embassy, too."

"I am very sorry about that," I repeated. "I'd had too much to drink and I also thought he was French. I wish he were here so I could apologize to him."

"I will tell him," she said with a little smile.

"You like this music?" I asked, gesturing toward the orchestra, which was playing "One O'Clock Jump."

"Very much," she said. "I come to listen to it whenever I can. It is really a kind of folk music."

"I know," I said. "I've become very fond of it myself. That is why I was here last night. I asked where I could hear some good jazz." I fumbled with the package I was carrying. "I wonder if I might give you a present?"

"What is it?" she asked.

"This," I said, showing the package. "I felt very bad about the way I acted last night. Even when I thought you were French, I wished to make amends. I thought you were a lover of jazz, so I brought you one of the records that I brought from America. Now, even more, I would like you to have it."

She took the package and unwrapped it. It was a record, on one side, of "Swingin' with Mezz," and on the other, "Dissonance." It had taken me a good part of the afternoon to find that record in Paris, but I'd succeeded.

She looked at it puzzled. "Mezz?" she asked.

"Mezz Mezzrow."

"Mezzrow? The one who plays here in Paris?"

I nodded. "This is one of his early records. It is very hard to find even in America."

For a minute I thought she was going to act like any other girl who has just gotten a nice present; I thought she was going to lean over and kiss me. Then she must have decided that wasn't the thing for a KGB agent to do, even to another agent, and she drew back just as she was starting to lean.

"Thank you," she said. "That's very nice of you. Is it the only one you have?"

"The only one of those two records, but I have many old jazz records that I'm taking home with me. I am glad that one will give you pleasure."

"Oh, it will," she said.

"I didn't think before," I said. "I should have introduced myself. I am Nikolai Menschivitch."

"I am Maryutka Kosygina." She smiled again.

We exchanged a few more remarks about jazz and then she excused herself to go to the ladies' room. That was where she said she was going, but I had an idea that she might be thinking of trying to check up on me. I felt surer about it when she returned, for she seemed preoccupied at first.

I called the waiter over and ordered drinks for both of us, remembering to make my French awkward and heavy with a Russian accent.

"To Moskva," I said to her when we had our drinks. She smiled and lifted her glass, and we drank to Moscow.

"It will be pleasant to be back in Moscow," I said. "The only thing to mar my pleasure is that all the girls I knew before I left are probably now married. Are you sure it isn't time for you to be going home on a vacation?"

"Quite sure," she said with a laugh.

"It is too bad," I said. I did my best to look like someone who was going to suffer from loneliness. "It would brighten my homecoming."

"There are plenty of our girls who will be glad to go out with a man such as you."

"Perhaps," I said, "but they will not share my interests. What a big difference it would make to know a girl I could sit around with and listen to the records I've brought back. With maybe a bottle of Stolichny vodka." She nodded.

"Can't you get sent back to report to the general?" I asked. I was referring to Serov, which was my only mention of her as an agent.

"I'm afraid not," she said. She was studying me and I could see she was debating with herself.

"Well," I said, "maybe I can get the general to introduce me to someone."

"You report directly to Serov?" she asked.

"Yes." I had a feeling that she was about to make a decision, so I didn't try to do any pushing.

Then she seemed to make up her mind. "I have a friend," she said, "who just went back home. Only I'm not sure how long she will stay there, since sooner or later she must come back to work in the Embassy here."

"Does she like jazz?" I asked.

"Yes. She used to come here with me all the time."

"Is she even partly as pretty as you are?"

"Oh, much prettier."

"Impossible," I exclaimed. "If she has one quarter of your beauty, I will be satisfied."

"She is much prettier," she said. "Her name is Zoya."

"A lovely name," I said. I also breathed a sigh of relief, but not so she could notice it.

"Zoya Aristova," she said. "You're leaving tonight? She will certainly be there for a few days and she will probably enjoy seeing you. She, too, has been away from Moscow for a long time. Not as long as you, but three years."

"She sounds delightful," I said. I tried to strike the right approach in my tone. Blind dates are pretty much the same the world over—you hope, but you also want a way out if she (or he) turns out to be a dog. So I tried to sound eager, but not too eager.

"You will like her," she said firmly. "Do you want to meet her?"

"Of course," I said. "Why would I not? If she is recommended by someone as pretty as you, then she must be very special."

"You have been too long in the bourgeois countries," she scolded, but it was obvious that she was secretly pleased. "She has a phone, so you can call her if you like. Her phone number is three-oh-five-six. She lives at Seven Kotelnicheskaya Embankment, block G, entrance F, apartment seventeen."

Fortunately I knew enough about Moscow to be impressed.

"One of the new apartment buildings," I exclaimed. "Who is your friend? A niece of Khrushchev?"

"She is a worker," Maryutka said piously, but there was a twinkle in her eye because, after all, we were comrades.

"Yes," I said solemnly. I reached into my coat and took out a pencil and paper and carefully wrote down—in Russian— all the information she had just given me. She repeated it carefully for me as I wrote.

"I will call her the minute I reach Moscow," I said. "May I give her a message from you?"

"Only that I envy her," she said with a smile. "I will imagine the two of you sitting and listening to your records or riding a river bus along the Moskva—but then it won't be too much longer until I have a holiday."

"Perhaps I can see you then," I said. "I don't know where I will be after I report, but I may learn before your friend returns to Paris, and if so, I will tell her and you can get in touch when you arrive."

"All right," she said.

After that we talked mostly about the music the orchestra was playing and I marked time. I had all I needed and wanted to get out, but I thought it wouldn't be a good idea to rush it. But I kept one eye on the time. When it was one o'clock I decided that I could make a break. That I'd better, in fact, because she'd be able to get her boss if she tried again.

I reassured her that I'd be waiting impatiently for her to come to Moscow and spent another five minutes saying good-bye, but then I got out and hurried up the stairs. There were several taxis parked at the stand. I went up to the first driver and handed him five thousand francs. I told him I wanted him to wait until a man appeared from the club and then to drive off in the general direction of the airport. If the man tried to follow him in another cab, he was to lose him. Five thousand francs was about fourteen dollars, so he was willing.

I went back and climbed into the next taxi and gave its driver his instructions. Then I settled back in the corner of the seat. I could see the entrance to the club, but it would be difficult for anyone to see me in the cab unless he leaned inside to look. Maybe I was being overly careful, but I didn't want to take any chances.

I didn't have long to wait. I'd barely settled back in the seat when he appeared in the doorway. There was no mistaking him. It was the same Russian who had been sitting with Maryutka the night before and whom I had glimpsed in the rear of the club earlier.

As he appeared, the cab ahead roared away from the curb. He hesitated a moment, peering after it, then came running straight for the taxi in which I sat.

FOUR

Pressing farther back into the corner of the cab, I watched as the Russian approached. He was just reaching for the door handle when my driver stopped him.

"I am waiting for someone, *m'sieu*," the driver said. "You will have to find another taxi."

He stopped for a minute, but I thought he was going to argue. Then he whirled and dashed back to the next taxi. He got in and it took off. But the first taxi was already far enough away so that I was sure the driver would have no trouble in evading the second one. I went back to watching the doorway.

Henri appeared almost at once. There was a worried look on his face as he stepped out on the street and looked around. I leaned forward and put my head out the window.

"Over here, Henri," I called.

He managed to look more worried and relieved at the same time. He came over to the taxi. "The other man," he said, "the one from last night, he just came up the stairs. I should have had him stopped, but he took me by surprise."

"I know," I said. "Get in and I'll tell you what happened to him while we're on our way."

He stepped into the cab; the driver took off. As we rode I explained what had happened to the Russian.

"You'd better check at the airport before I show up, however," I said.

"It's possible that he will go on there after he loses the cab. He didn't have much time to talk to the girl, but she may have told him that I was supposed to be taking the Russian plane. He might check with the pilot."

"He stopped and exchanged a few words with the girl on his way out," Henri said.

"I don't think she was suspicious," I said, "although in the beginning I think she may have tried to call and check up on me. Even so, with her training, she probably wouldn't object if he wanted to check. And her friend probably remembers the punch in the jaw I gave him last night."

"It went all right with her?"

"I think so. She gave me the address and the phone number of the other girl. I suppose it's possible she gave me phony ones, but I don't think so."

"She'll soon wish that she had," Henri said. "He'll check the airport and she'll probably check with Belyayev. He in turn may call Moscow. If so, they'll certainly know that you are not a Russian agent and they will then jump to the right conclusion. They'll probably put a ring of agents around the girl in Moscow and warn her, too."

"Maybe," I said, "but I sort of doubt it. The girl may not want anyone to know that she was duped into giving any information and so she may keep her mouth shut about that part of it. Perhaps not even warn her friend. But even if she does, it will be all right."

"How?"

"I have no intention of approaching the girl either as an agent or as a friend of this girl in Paris. Now that I have her address, I'll find another way to get to her. If I'm lucky, it won't make any difference if they do have other agents watching her."

The taxi pulled up in front of my hotel. Henri and I went in and collected my things, then checked out. We caught another taxi to the airport.

"All right, what is your plan, my friend?" Henri asked when the taxi was under way.

"I don't have any," I said cheerfully.

"*Mon Dieu!* It is not possible. You must have some plan."

"Not really. I have a rough idea of something that might work, but I won't know until I can take a look around in East Germany. Until then there's no point in talking about it."

"Do we go over to take the look this morning?"

"Not we," I said. "Me. All you have to do is stay on the western side and be prepared for anything I may come up with."

He swore softly. "How can I be prepared when I don't know what I'm preparing for?"

I grinned at him. "I'm sure you will find a way, my friend. I know how talented you are."

"*Sale bête,*" he said.

Then we were at the airport. I stayed in the cab while Henri went to take a look. He soon came back to report that the Russian was nowhere in sight. He'd also checked and the Russian plane had taken off. We paid off the driver and went into the terminal, but we then went directly to the plane that was waiting to take us to Germany. As soon as we were aboard the pilot took off.

Knowing that it would be a busy day, I slept most of the way to Berlin. We landed shortly after four-thirty in the morning. We were met by David Farley, the CIA man in West Berlin. I had met him a few years before when I had been there. We'd liked each other, so it was nice seeing him again.

Again, it didn't take long to clear through the official channels, and then the three of us drove through Berlin to the CIA offices. The streets were mostly deserted at that hour. I could see as we rode along that there had been a lot more rebuilding of the city since I was last there.

We did no talking until we were up in the CIA offices. We went into Farley's private office and turned on the lights. He opened a box of cigarettes and pushed them across the desk.

"Nothing stronger?" I asked.

"Sorry," he said, smiling. "Can you imagine what a congressman back home would say if he found out that I served liquor in the office? Especially in the early hours of the morning."

"He'd probably make a speech, in between sips of bourbon," I admitted. "Oh, well, I'll suffer for my country and Dulles."*

"It's a good thing my security officer isn't here," Farley said dryly. "Now, what's the program, March? All I know is that

---

* John Foster Dulles, a controversial Secretary of State under President Dwight Eisenhower, was aggressively opposed to Communism, which he condemned for its "evil" atheism. A moralistic stance is one of the attributes that most triggers Milo's sarcasm. This novel was published in February 1959, and Dulles died of cancer the following May.

you're out to recover something and that I have orders to put everything aside if necessary in order to assist you. In other words, the whole office is yours."

"Thanks for nothing," I said. "So far there isn't any program. So a boy in Paris went overboard for a pair of pretty gams and gave her a paper that was more loaded than he knew. Washington is in an uproar and wants the paper back. In the meantime, the pair of pretty gams has decamped for Russia. Now all that I'm supposed to do is go to Russia and get it back."

He whistled softly. "That's some assignment."

"It's all right," I said. "The only trouble is that I don't like caviar and I always did think that vodka was inferior to gin."

"How are you going to do it?"

"He doesn't know," Henri said. "He's going to—how does one say it in the American thrillers?—play it on his ear."

"It's 'by ear,' Henri," I told him. "But it's not quite like that. I have a rough idea, but I'll have to check on it today. I'm going over to East Berlin. If my idea will work out, then we'll have to move fast. Actually, I'd prefer not to talk too much about it, for two reasons. One, it isn't developed yet. Two, I'm not sure that even the CIA will approve of every bit of it."

Henri's face brightened at the news, but Farley looked harassed. "If you're sure about that," he said, "maybe you'd better not tell me."

I grinned at him. "I wasn't going to. In the meantime, there are a couple of things you can be doing while I'm in East Berlin. For one thing, I'll need money. Quite a bit of it, since it may be difficult to draw on anyone for cash once I'm in Russia."

"I've already gotten orders to give you unlimited funds," Farley said. "So far as I know, it's the first time that's ever happened."

"I'll need some Eastern marks," I said, "and I guess the rest in rubles."

"You'd better try to take dollars. For Russia, that is. You can get an official rate now of about ten rubles to the dollar, but you'll be able to get fourteen or fifteen to the dollar on the black market in Moscow. You won't do as well with marks as you will with dollars."

I thought about it a minute. It might have advantages to work with dollars, enough to offset the disadvantages. "Okay," I said. "I'll take your advice on it."

"How much do you want?"

"Better let me have about four thousand marks," I said. "I'll need that this morning, within four or five hours."

"That I can do," he said. "I have that much here. I'll give it to you before you leave. How much in dollars?"

"I have no way of knowing how much I will need," I said. "The big problem is going to be getting out of Russia. I don't suppose that anyone is going to give me a list of people in Russia who might help me?"

"I don't even have such a list," Farley said. "And I haven't had any orders about it."

"I thought so," I said. "So March is on his own. That may mean that I have to buy a few people. Better make it at least ten thousand dollars."

He winced, but that was all. "I'll have it for you by tonight. Will that be soon enough?"

I nodded. "Now, another thing. There is one aspect of my idea which you had better not be a part of. If you just give some help without asking any questions, I think that Henri will supply the rest of it. You don't mind breaking a few rules, do you, Henri?"

"No," he said happily.

"Don't even tell me you're going to break them," Farley said. "I don't want to know anything about it. What is it you want me to do?"

"Henri will need a house. It can be small, but it should be in a fairly isolated section where he won't be bothered with neighbors. He should have it and be moved in by tonight."

Farley thought for a minute. "I can manage that, I guess. It'll be ready by tonight."

"I guess that's all from you," I said. "Unless something goes wrong with my original idea."

He sighed with relief. "You're letting me off more easily than I expected. If you get a chance while you're in Moscow, you might do a little favor for all of us."

"Sure, it's going to be like a vacation," I said ironically. "What's the favor?"

"The Russians have one agent who's been driving all of us crazy. And I do mean all. In every part of Europe. All you have to do is find out who she is while you're there and a lot of us will stop aging."

"She?"

"Yes. As near as we know she's been operating all over Europe for the past year or so. We know her code name and that's all."

"What is it?"

"Rozenka."

"The Rose," I translated. "Well, if I get chummy with Serov, I'll ask him. Now, if you don't mind I'd like to go get two or three hours' sleep before I take off."

"Of course," he said. He got up and went over to his office safe. He opened it and took out a bundle of mark notes. I could see they were East German marks. He counted off some and pushed them toward me. "Four thousand marks," he said. "I'll have to ask you to sign for them."

"Naturally. We mustn't let the congressmen think we're wasting money." I waited until he got out a form and filled it out. Then I signed it.

"Henri will keep in touch," I said. "It'll probably be better if I don't come around too much. Well, keep them flying."

"Good luck," he said. He held out his hand and I shook it. Then Henri and I left. We quickly found a hotel and registered. With a little talking I also managed to get a drink. Then we went up to the room. Henri wanted to talk, but I told him to wake me up in three hours and then we'd talk. I was asleep as soon as I put my head on the pillow.

It was nine o'clock when Henri awakened me. I had a waiter come up with a pot of strong coffee and a bottle of whiskey. After two cups of coffee and three drinks of the whiskey, I lit a cigarette and looked at Henri.

"There's not much to it," I said. "In about fifteen or twenty minutes I'm going over to the Soviet section. You'd better go to work on getting that house through Farley. Also pick up the money. Maybe you'd better not sign for it. Get him to give you the form and I'll sign when I see you. That way, you won't appear in this operation just in case anything backfires with the part you will play. You still have your Berlin connections?"

"You mean the ones who thought I was a black market operator?" he asked. "Yes. Why?"

. "You may or may not need some help. If you have time, get in touch with them just for old time's sake; then, if you need them, you can call on them. Be back here at the hotel by six tonight and wait for me to phone or show up. If I phone, it may be from the Eastern zone, so watch your language."

"I wish you'd tell me what you're up to," he said.

"You'll worry less if you don't know. If everything goes all right, you'll have your work cut out for you, so don't blow your stack." I finished my coffee and snubbed the cigarette out. I stood up. "Okay, Henri. Keep the home fires burning."

"Bonne chance," he said. "I'll be here, mon vieux."

"I know you will," I told him. "Otherwise, I'd be worrying." I grinned at him and left the room without looking back.

I left the hotel and took a cab to Gleisdreieck. I went down into the subway and took the first train going east. There weren't many people in the train and most of them were heavily shawled women who had probably taken the risk of crossing over to the west to shop. The next stop was Potsdamer Platz, which is right on the border between West Berlin and East Berlin. Everybody got off the car except the women shoppers and me. No one paid any attention to me. The doors closed and the train slid back into its dark tunnel. We were in Communist Germany.

I stayed on the train until we reached Alexander Platz. I went upstairs and went to the HO store.* I bought everything new from the skin out. Underwear, socks, shoes, shirt, tie, and suit. When I left the store I went to a public bathhouse and changed clothes. I checked my old clothes carefully to make sure there were no identifying labels or marks and wrapped them up. I went back to the subway and took a train headed for the west. I stayed on until we reached Potsdamer Platz, then got off, leaving the package of old clothes on the train. That way, it would be found in the west zone and the East Berlin police wouldn't be on a special lookout for an agent.

I crossed over and took another train back to East Berlin. This time I rode to the Spittelmarkt station. As I left the station, I passed a huge poster showing two Germans in the uniforms of the People's Police and the State Security Police. Below, in red letters, was the legend *Die deutsche Volkspolizei ist das Blut vom Blut des deutschen Volkes.*** I secretly thumbed my nose at the poster and went on.

It didn't take me long to find out where the trade meetings were being held. It was only a few blocks away, so I walked over. It was in one of the new buildings they had built. The flag of every Iron Curtain country was flying over the entrance. The meetings were open to the public, so I had no trouble getting in.

The main hall was crowded with several hundred men and women. The front part was taken up by delegates and the last half with observers. There were about two dozen men

---

* *HO* stands for Handels-Organisation, or Trade Organization, a state-owned department store of East Germany.
** "The German People's Police is the blood of the blood of the German people."

seated on the stage. I recognized a couple of them. One was General Ivan Alexandrovich Serov, the head of the Russian secret police. The other was Anastas Mikoyan, First Deputy Premier of the Soviet Union. There were also several German Communists I recognized, including the head of the East German secret police.

A heavyset Hungarian was speaking, his speech being translated into German and Russian by two interpreters. The gist of his remarks was that Hungary hadn't produced much in the past year because of the interference by capitalist warmongers but that the next year they would be on the ball.

I stayed in the rear of the hall for several minutes looking over the delegates. There were signs indicating where each group was from. The Russians were all at one side, with signs showing which one of the Russian republics they were from. There were more Russians than any other nationality, but I soon noticed that most of them were from the larger republics. Over to one side they had the delegates from the Georgian, Armenian, and Azerbaijan republics lumped together. There were only three of them, one from each republic, and they looked pretty much as if they were being left out of things. I finally went over and found a seat directly back of them.

One of them was an old man and I ignored him. The other two looked to be about my age. They seemed to have nothing in common except their geographical kinship, for they seldom glanced at each other or exchanged any words. Finally a name was called from the stage and one of them got up and walked to the front.

He started a speech, in Russian with a strong Azerbaijanese accent, about the oil and cotton production in his republic. The figures were fairly impressive, but that was about all you could say for the speech. After he'd reeled off the facts, he launched into a short explanation. It was true, he said, that the government had recently published a four-year production cycle for the new pipe rolling mill in Baku, but the mill was not yet built and couldn't go into production until it was. The wooers of Azerbaijan, however, were applying themselves with true socialist zeal, and it should soon be built.

There was slight applause when he finished and he plodded back to his seat, looking as if he was glad it was over.

I had been studying him carefully as he spoke. He wasn't quite as tall as I and was maybe a little stockier, but I was deciding that he was my man if he could only pass the rest of the test.

The speeches droned on and on, all of them getting polite applause, although no one seemed to be paying much attention. A man sitting next to me leaned over and whispered in German that Khrushchev was going to speak the next day. I answered him in Russian and that ended the conversation.

Finally it became apparent that they were about to break for lunch. I got up and made my way back to the entrance. I waited until the session was formally ended, then I went outside to wait.

The delegates soon began to straggle out, mostly in little groups, but from what I could make out from the languages and accents, they were still sticking together according to nationality or section. The three men I had been watching came out together but separated without a word to each other. The one who interested me went down the street alone. I followed at a leisurely pace.

We walked six or seven blocks and then came to the Neva Restaurant, which he entered. I knew the restaurant from the time I'd been in East Berlin before. It featured many Russian foods and liquors and was a great favorite of many of the East Berlin Communists, but so far as I knew, Russians seldom went there. I waited a few minutes and then entered.

It was reasonably crowded. Looking around, I spotted the man I'd been following. He was sitting alone and I felt better, for I'd been afraid that he was on his way to meet someone. There was another empty table next to him and I went over and took it. He was just finishing his order as I sat down.

I ordered a glass of Stolichny vodka and a large plate of *solyanka,* which is a Russian meat soup. I noticed my neighbor watching me as I ordered, but I paid no attention. When the waiter brought my vodka, I got out a cigarette and fumbled for a match. Not finding one, I snapped my fingers for the waiter, who had already retreated beyond hearing.

"Vot zagigalka," my neighbor said.

I looked around in apparent surprise, then leaned over to light my cigarette from the lighter he held. *"Bolshoe spasibo,"* I said. I took a closer look at him. "Oh," I continued in Russian, "you were one of the speakers this morning, weren't you?"

He nodded, looking delighted. "You are a Russian?" he asked.

"Of course," I said. "Nikolai Menschivitch."

"Mikhail Kirilenko," he said, introducing himself. "You are also a delegate?"

"No," I said. "I work here in Germany. It is a terrible place, but the money is good and one must do it."

A shadow passed over his face and I knew what he was thinking. I hastened to correct it. "I am an engineer," I said. "Here to teach the stupid Germans how they should do things."

The shadow passed from his face and I knew I had guessed right. When I had told him I worked in Germany, his first thought had been that I was with the MVD or the secret police. The average Russian is like the citizen of any other country; he doesn't like to socialize with secret policemen.

"You have been here long?" he asked politely.

"Five years," I said. "Too long. I miss our country. You are from Baku, are you not?"

He nodded again. "How did you know?"

"Your accent," I said. "For a short time I worked in your republic." I added the last sentences in Azerbaijanese. That one sentence was about the extent of my knowledge of that language, but it delighted him.

We talked throughout lunch and I found out most of the things I wanted to know.

He knew the other delegates only slightly and he was glad to have company. As soon as this meeting was over, after Khrushchev spoke the next day, he was to go on to the larger trade meeting in Moscow. He was already booked on a flight taking off an hour after the Berlin meeting was over. He had his ticket and a reservation at the Hotel National in Moscow.

He was looking forward to the visit, for he had never been to Moscow before.

By the time lunch was over we were fast friends, calling each other Mikhail and Nikolai, and we had made a date to meet that evening and have dinner together. I explained that I was going to be busy that afternoon and couldn't attend the trade meeting, so we arranged to meet at his hotel that evening at seven. He was staying at the Lenin Hotel. He left then to go back to the meeting, and I stayed in the restaurant to have a couple more drinks, switching to brandy.

Things had progressed faster and better than I had dared hope that morning, so I had the afternoon free. One good thing about it was that I wouldn't have to phone that evening from East Berlin. It was usually pretty safe, but there was no way to tell when the operators might listen in. I left the restaurant and took the subway back to the Western section. When I got there, I phoned the CIA and got Farley on the phone. I asked him if he knew where I could reach Henri. He said he was expecting to hear from Henri any minute and I should phone back in about fifteen minutes. I told him to have Henri name a place where he could meet me. I hunted up a bar and had a couple more drinks. Then I called back. Henri had left word that he would meet me in the Flasche Café on Mehring Platz at once.

I took a taxi to Mehring Platz and found the café without any trouble. Henri had a corner table and was waiting. There was a bottle of brandy and two glasses on the table.

"You must be planning on a big afternoon," I said, indicating the bottle as I sat down.

"Compliments of the house," he said. "How could I say no? The proprietor still thinks I'm a big man in black market activities, and he wants to be sure that I remember him with kindness. Don't tell me that you have become so softened by civilian life that a bottle of brandy frightens you?"

"Hardly," I said. I poured myself a generous drink. "But it may be too rich for my blood. I've been drinking Russian brandy."

Henri was looking me over. "New clothes, too," he said. "What did you do with the old ones?"

"Left them on a subway in West Berlin."

He grinned. "They'll end up in the offices of the West Berlin secret police and they'll be combing the city for a spy."

"Good," I said. "What's happened since I left this morning?"

He gave me a scornful glance. "You expect miracles, *mon vieux?* You are gone perhaps four hours and come back and expect everything to be the way you want it? Well, I have your money for you."

"What about the house?" I asked.

"I have that, too."

"How does it look?"

He threw up his hands in mock horror. "I'm supposed to have looked at it, too? Maybe I should have ordered new carpets? *Pour l'amour de Dieu!*"

"What does it look like, Henri?" I repeated.

"It's all right," he said sourly. "It's isolated enough for almost anything. The trouble with you is that you expect the impossible and then everybody produces it for you."

"Sure," I said. I grinned at him. "You see, I know you. If it were anyone else, I wouldn't expect anything. But I knew you'd be out one minute after I left the hotel. Tell me the truth. You had everything ready and sized up two hours ago, didn't you?"

"It was only an hour ago," he said reluctantly. "What do we do now?"

"Be there by eight o'clock tonight. I'll probably arrive around nine, but it might be earlier and it might be later. Get me some knockout drops or pills. Wait for me."

"Alone?"

"Me?" I asked. "I hope not. If I am, all will be lost. Among your many old friends, I don't suppose there would be one who could take care of a hot car?"

"There might be. From the East?"

I nodded. "We'll give it to him to make it more appealing."

"No. That would only make him suspicious. We'll sell it to him cheap. What kind of car?"

"How the hell do I know?" I asked. "I haven't stolen it yet. Just have your friend standing by to take it quickly."

"Yes, Your Majesty," he said dryly. "You're still not going to tell me what's going on?"

"Not yet. We'll pretend it's going to be your birthday."

"Maybe I will go into the black market," he said darkly. "At least I'll be well paid there."

"Ah, but there you will be only another Frenchman," I told him. "Now give me the address of the house."

He wrote it down on a piece of paper and passed it over to me. I glanced at it and saw that I knew roughly how to find it. I tucked it away in my pocket. "One for the road," I said, pouring myself another drink of brandy. I tossed it off. "Well, I will see you, Henri."

"You're not even going to stay to help me finish the bottle?" he said. "Some friend."

"You're going to finish the bottle?"

"Certainly," he said with dignity. "Never let it be said that a Frenchman was intimidated by a bottle of brandy. Especially one that is on the house."

"Okay, Henri. I'll see you sometime tonight."

"All right," he said. He was sitting and staring belligerently at the bottle of brandy as I left.

I took the subway back to East Berlin and got off at Alexander Platz. I still had a few hours to kill, so I bought a paper and went to the nearest café. There wasn't much of interest in the paper. At least half of it was taken up with the fact that Khrushchev had arrived in East Berlin. He was staying at Karlshorst—which in official sources was called the Little Kremlin. He would make a speech the following day before returning to Moscow. There were pictures of Khrushchev arriving at the airport, Khrushchev riding in his car through the streets of Berlin, Khrushchev patting a little girl on the head, Khrushchev having a glass of German beer. He looked just like a politician running for office—only he didn't have to run for any office.

Everything else in the paper was just as phony as Khrushchev's smile, and I finally gave up on it. I sat around in the café until it was time to go meet my new friend at his hotel. The Lenin Hotel wasn't far away, and I walked to it. Mikhail

Kirilenko was already there and waiting for me. He reported that everything had gone well at the trade meeting that afternoon and then we dropped the subject. We went downstairs to the dining room in the hotel.

Now that the day was over, Kirilenko was apparently ready to relax. We both ordered vodka and then the toasts started. We drank to the president of the Azerbaijan Soviet Socialist Republic, the president of the Russian Soviet Socialist Republic, the mayor of Baku, Khrushchev, and Mikoyan. After that we just drank. By the time we got around to food, Kirilenko was well on his way to being stoned and I wasn't doing too badly myself.

The vodka kept coming while we ate, and I'm still not quite sure what we had for dinner. When we had finally finished coffee, with more vodka, I suggested that we take a walk. He agreed. At the moment, I had nothing in mind but going out and getting some fresh air. But once we were on the street, I had a bright idea, one I would have quickly shunned if I hadn't drunk so much vodka. I went ahead and suggested that we walk past Karlshorst and see if we could get a glimpse of Khrushchev. Kirilenko was just drunk enough to agree. So off we went.

There was nothing to see in front of Karlshorst except a generous supply of MVD men and the German secret police, and we didn't linger in front of the building. We rounded the corner of the building, and suddenly there was an empty street which looked very welcome. The street was lined with big cars, and in front there was a black Zis. The others cars were all of German make, so I guessed the Zis was the one that they were using for Khrushchev. I was still full enough of vodka to want to go ahead with the brainstorm I'd had when we left the hotel.

"Look at it," I said, stopping beside the Zis. "Look how superior it is to those German cars."

"It must be a wonderful car," Kirilenko said. You could tell by his tone that he hoped someday he would be important enough to ride in a Zis, but that he also knew there was little chance. The Zis was reserved for very important customers in Russia; others had to be content with a Zim, or something smaller.

"Would you like to ride in it?" I asked him.

He turned to face me in astonishment. "You joke, of course?" he said.

"*Nyet,*" I said. "*Izvinite.*" With that apology, I hit him as hard as I could. My fist connected solidly with his jaw, and the expression of surprise was wiped from his face. His knees buckled and he started to slide to the sidewalk. I grabbed him beneath the arms and looked around. The street was still deserted. I dragged him over to the Zis, opened the rear door, and shoved him inside. I closed the door, then went around and got in behind the wheel.

There was no key, of course, but it took only a minute to tear loose the ignition wires and fasten them together. I stepped on the starter and the motor roared into life.

"Sorry, Mikhail, old friend," I said. "You're getting your wish, but you'll never remember it." I put the car in gear and the big Zis surged forward smoothly and powerfully.

FIVE

By the time I'd driven five or six blocks, I was beginning to wish that I hadn't had so much vodka-courage and had stolen a less important car. Every time I came to a policeman he would glance at the license plate and then salute. I didn't mind being saluted, but I didn't like being so conspicuous. The whole idea was enough to sober me up quickly. But then, when I was more sober, I decided that the scheme wasn't so bad after all. If the theft of the car wasn't discovered too quickly, it might make the whole thing easier.

It turned out that way. In no time at all, ignoring such things as speed limits, I was at Brandenburg Gate and the dividing line between East and West Berlin. The Communist guards at the gate looked surprised at the sight of the car crossing over but quickly snapped to attention and saluted. Then I was in West Berlin.

That presented another problem. The West German police might just as easily recognize the car and they wouldn't salute; they'd be more apt to stop it. So I switched off of Unter den Linden and started using small side streets. It slowed me up some, but not too much, and in about forty minutes I was on the street where Henri had the house. I drove slowly, peering out the window, until I spotted the number. It was a small white house with plenty of space between it and other houses. I stopped in front of it and cut the lights. I disconnected the wires and the motor died.

There was a groan from the back seat. My Russian friend was starting to come around. I got out quickly and opened the back door. I leaned in and chopped across the side of his neck with the edge of my hand. He went limp and the groaning stopped. I closed the door and went to the house. I knocked on the door. A moment later the door opened and Henri looked out.

"So, it's you," he said. "Alone?"

"No," I said. "Keep the door open and wait." I turned and went back to the car. I checked first and the street was empty. I opened the door and dragged Kirilenko out. I closed the door and threw him over my shoulder. I went back to the house. Henri was still holding the door open. I stepped inside and he closed it.

"You should be more careful about the friends you pick," he said. "Is he drunk?"

"No," I said. I tossed him onto the couch. "Knocked out. I just knocked him out for the second time. This one ought to last ten minutes or so. There's a car out front. No key, but the wires are loose and can be put together so it'll run. Maybe you ought to call your friend and have him take it away quickly."

Henri looked at me. "This car," he said. "It wouldn't just happen to be a Russian Zis, would it?"

"Strangely enough, it is," I said. "Why?"

"Three minutes ago there was a broadcast from the East Berlin radio saying that the Zis especially reserved for the use of the illustrious visitor Nikita S. Khrushchev had just been stolen by some capitalistic criminal."

"What a coincidence," I murmured.

"Dont les couilles étaient vraiment immenses," he exclaimed.

"I was drunk," I explained, "and it seemed a good idea at the moment. This character kept offering toasts. In the meantime, you'd better get your friend busy and get rid of the car before the West Berlin police start asking questions. We probably could explain it to them, but I'd hate to have to."

"A Zis, eh?" he said. "New?"

"I guess so. There's only ten thousand kilometers on it."

He got up and went to the phone. He dialed a number and waited. "Gerhardt," he said finally. "Henri. We've got the car, but if you want it, you have to pick it up in fifteen minutes. It's a Zis—the private car of a very important man who is now on the front pages—so it will cost you an additional four thousand marks. ... All right. Tomorrow. Pick it up in front of the address I gave you. In fifteen minutes. The ignition wires are loose. Just twist them together. ... Good. I'll see you tomorrow." He hung up.

"What are you going to do with the additional thousand dollars?" I asked.

He looked at me with a pained expression. "It's a private matter," he said. "What would your American Congress say if the CIA was to receive a thousand dollars from a stolen car? Why, it might even overthrow the republic."

"It might upset a few people," I admitted.

"What would your Mr. Dulles do?"

"Blow a gasket, probably. All right, Henri, I will not mention sordid money again. Your friend will pick up the car?"

"Within fifteen minutes," he said. He gestured toward the man on the couch. "What about this one?"

"You," I said, "are to hold him prisoner until I get out of Russia."

"That's all?" he asked sourly.

"That's all," I said cheerfully. "Once I'm out, you can send him back to Russia or turn him over to the CIA in the event that he's decided by that time he'd rather stay here. Okay?"

"Do I have a choice?" he asked sarcastically.

"No," I confessed. I went over and started going through Kirilenko's pockets. There were all kinds of identification: his credentials as a trade delegate for Azerbaijan, his identity card for his home republic, his internal passport that permitted him to travel in greater Russia, his Communist Party card, and so on. Several of them had his picture on them, but they were like most passport pictures; if no one looked too closely, they would look like pictures of me. I took everything that was in his pockets except his money and the pictures of his family. Those I put back.

"What do we do with him?" I asked.

"It might help," Henri said, "if you didn't make me be a mind reader all the time. However, I did fix up the master bedroom ..." He walked across the room and threw open a door. I could see a small bedroom with one window that was barred. "He can't get out," Henri continued. "The first two or three screams won't be heard, and by that time I can reach him."

"Good," I said. "Did it come that way?"

"Are you joking?" he asked scornfully. "I had the bars put

on the window this afternoon. The bottle of brandy that was on the house helped. I sat and thought, and it came to me that you were going to kidnap someone and then ask me to guard him. *Voilà!* I put up the bars."

"You see," I told him. "I don't have to tell you what is going to happen. You do the right things anyway."

"Je m'en fous," he exclaimed. "Bring in the guest."

I picked up the Russian and carried him into the bedroom, dropping him gently on the bed. I loosened his tie so that he could breathe easier. When I finally straightened up, Henri was standing beside me, a hypodermic in his hand.

"I took other precautions," he said. "This will keep him out until tomorrow morning."

"What is it?"

"Pentothal. It won't hurt him, but it will keep him quiet for the night. Tomorrow is another day."

"Okay," I said. I waited while Henri gave him the injection, and then we went back into the other room, closing the door to the bedroom. We had barely sat down when we heard the sound of a starting motor in front of the house.

"Ah, that's my friend," Henri said. "He has picked up the car. So you see, you can relax."

"Sure. And in twenty-four hours I'll be in Russia and then I can relax more."

"You are going to become him?" Henri asked, nodding toward the bedroom.

I nodded. "We are close enough in size to make it possible. Also he is the only delegate from his republic and apparently did not become very friendly with any of the other delegates.

That's what I went looking for. I figured that there would be single delegates from the smaller republics. It's not the safest thing in the world, but it's safer than any other way I could think of."

"What about the meeting tomorrow?"

"I won't show up. I'll have a cold or something. It may not be smart, since Khrushchev is the high point of tomorrow's meeting, but the party functionaries will probably be so busy they won't notice too much. Then I'll take his plane reservation, and it should put me in Moscow a few hours before General Serov gets there. Those few hours will tell the story of whether I get back the paper or not."

"Then how do you get out?" Henri asked soberly.

"One thing at a time," I said. "I'll worry about that after I get there and after I get the paper—if I do. I will have to play it—how do you say it in French?—on the ear."

He grinned at me. "I wish I were going with you, *mon vieux*."

"If I were going to have anybody with me, I'd rather have you than anyone else," I told him. I meant it, too. "Well, I guess I'd better get started. Got money for me?"

He nodded and pulled a bulky envelope from his pocket. "There's a receipt inside with the money that Farley wants you to sign."

"And I'll bet somewhere in Washington there's an accountant who will make me explain where every penny of it went," I said. I unsealed the envelope and pulled the wad of bills from it. I counted them. Ten thousand dollars. Exactly. "Wouldn't you think," I asked as I signed the form, "that just once sometime they'd make a mistake and put in one extra dollar?"

"Impossible," he said. "Anyone who works for a government agency must have the built-in ability never to make such a mistake. An undercount might be permissible, but to give away government money is unthinkable. You should know better, my friend."

"I do—but I can hope, can't I? Well, Henri, I'll be seeing you."

"I hope so."

"I will," I told him with a grin. "Take care of our friend. As soon as I'm out of Russia, I'll send you word and you can put him on a subway for East Berlin, if he still wants to go, or you can pack him off to the CIA if he'd rather have that. I think by that time he may decide that he doesn't want to go back to Russia. They probably frown heavily on delegates who let themselves be kidnapped and impersonated. So long, Henri."

"*Au revoir, mon vieux,*" he said. "Give my regards to the Red Square."

I grinned at him and left. I walked about five blocks before I found a subway station. I had to change trains once, but I was soon back in East Berlin. I went straight to Kirilenko's hotel and used his key to let myself into his room.

I spent the next couple of hours taking an inventory. He had brought considerable clothing with him and practically all of it fit me. Not perfectly, but well enough.

There were various kinds of trade papers and reports and a copy of a speech that must have been intended for Moscow. On the dresser there was a picture of a woman I imagined was his wife and a half-finished letter to her. I wondered how long it would be before she would start asking about him. Not that it made any difference. I had no illusion about lasting that long as Mikhail Kirilenko. I certainly couldn't expect to get away with it at the trade meetings. The seating arrangements would probably be similar to those at the Berlin meeting, and the two delegates who had been seated with him would know I wasn't the right man. Even though Kirilenko hadn't been friendly with any other delegates, there might be dozens who at least knew him by sight.

So far as my impersonation was concerned, it probably couldn't last more than one or two days. I might stretch it a little by pretending to be sick and staying in my hotel room, but I doubted if that would work long. Still, it would be good long enough; if I didn't get the paper at once, there wouldn't be any more chances. If I was lucky, I might be able to travel through a large part of Russia as Kirilenko because it might be a few days before they sent out any sort of general alarm for him.

That was my best bet, and I didn't think it was too far-fetched. There probably were delegates who got drunk and vanished for a day or two, so maybe no one would pay any attention if Kirilenko didn't show up at once. When they did get concerned, they might first just have the police look for him in Moscow. So there ought to be another three days before the search would branch out. If everything went smoothly, that would give me about four days, or a little longer, to travel on Kirilenko's internal passport.

The more I thought about it, the better it seemed. Barring an accident, I wouldn't have to worry about getting out immediately. I could just concentrate on Zoya Aristova.

Having checked the possessions in the room and gone over the approach in my mind, I undressed and went to bed. I was asleep almost at once.

I was up fairly early the following morning. I checked through Kirilenko's papers and found the name of the chairman of the Berlin conference. I went downstairs and had breakfast not far from the hotel. Then I phoned the hall where the meetings were being held. I wasn't able to get the chairman to the phone, but I left a message saying that Mikhail Kirilenko was indisposed and would not be at the morning meeting.

After breakfast, I bought the papers and a small bottle of brandy and went back to the hotel room. The papers were again filled with news of the visit of Khrushchev. There was also a small story about the theft of the car that had been assigned to the visiting Russian premier, with a strong hint that the whole thing had been a plot by the Americans and the British.

I spent the rest of the morning and the early part of the afternoon in the room, reading the papers and drinking the brandy. Then I packed and went down and checked out in the name of Mikhail Kirilenko. There were no problems. All they knew was his name and all they wanted was his money.

I took a cab to the airfield and checked in for the flight to Moscow. The big Russian jet plane was waiting on the field, and it didn't take long before I was cleared through and going aboard. The plane was filling up with delegates, and

I was aware that there was a certain risk involved, but not too much. Several of the men glanced at me curiously as if they were trying to place me, but that was all. There wasn't even any name tag to identify me, so all they could do was speculate. And, fortunately, neither of the two men who had flanked Kirilenko was booked on the same flight with me.

Finally the plane was loaded and it took off. I exchanged a few words with my seat companion, who was voluble in stating that he was a delegate from the Estonian Soviet Socialist Republic. At last I managed to cut him off and I went to sleep.

Three hours later I awakened as the plane came down on the field in Moscow. A Zis limousine took us into the city. Part of the delegates were dropped off at a hotel, and then the rest of us were driven on to the Hotel National.

After a short wait, my papers were looked at and I was shown upstairs to my room. I hadn't been certain that I would have a room to myself, but I did. In fact, it was a large, pleasant room. The rug and the walls were shabby in spots, but it was clean. There were heavy red velvet curtains. There was also an old-fashioned desk with a deep square glass ashtray and an inkwell and pen. I noticed that the ink was purple.

I went over and pulled the curtains back from the windows. The windows were carefully sealed against the cold with tape, but there were little trap windows through which fresh air came into the room. My room was in the front of the hotel, and from the window there was a magnificent view of the Kremlin, the illuminated red stars atop the towers moving slowly and majestically in the wind.

But there wasn't much time to admire the view. It was still

early evening, even though it was dark, but before long it would be too late for my purpose. I put away my things and left the room. I went out on Manezhnaya Square and walked down the street until I came to a public phone booth. I went in and deposited fifteen kopecks and dialed the number the girl in Paris had given me. On the third ring she answered. Her voice was soft and rich. I hung up without saying anything and left the phone booth.

I was on Gorky Street, the main street running through Moscow, and I kept walking along it, watching. I had a rough idea where I needed to go and felt pretty confident that I would recognize the people I wanted when I saw them. Black market operators are pretty much of a breed all over the world.

I had gone five or six blocks before I saw a group of youths wearing clothes that looked as if they might have come from America. I had never seen any of them before, but I was certain they were what was known as the *stilyagi*—Moscow's equivalent of hipsters. They might be part of my answer.

There were five of them strolling aimlessly along the street ahead of me. I quickened my pace and caught up with them.

"*Zdravstvuyte,*" I said. "I am a stranger in Moscow. Can you tell me where I could sell American dollars for rubles?"

The five of them stopped and stared at me. None of them said anything for a minute while they carefully looked me over. They may have wondered if I was from the police, but they showed no fear.

"Where did you get dollars?" one of them asked.

"I have them," I said. "If you can direct me to the proper

place to sell them, I will give you ten dollars to divide among you. After I have made the transaction."

There was another hesitation. I think they were trying to decide if they should just knock me out and take all that I had. I shifted my position slightly to be ready for whatever happened.

"How do we know that you are not of the police?" one of them wanted to know.

"You don't," I said. I pulled a few American bills from my pocket. "But who would trust a policeman with such money?"

They laughed at that and the atmosphere changed. "All right," said one of them. "Come with us."

We cut down one of the side streets and walked a couple more blocks, ending up in front of a small restaurant. There was a shabby-looking man standing in front of it.

"We have brought you a customer, Nuritdin," one of them said.

He looked me over. "What do you want?" he asked.

"Rubles," I said.

"For what?"

"American dollars."

An interested gleam came into his eyes. "Let us take a walk," he said.

We started strolling down the street, with the five youths sauntering along behind us.

"How many dollars?" he asked.

"How many can you buy?" I asked.

He shrugged.

"Five hundred dollars?" I asked.

"I could manage," he said. "Twelve rubles for the dollar."

"No good," I said. "I can get ten by going to the state bank, so I should have more than twelve."

"They will want to know where you got the dollars if you go to the bank. I do not ask questions."

"Let them want to know," I said. "I want seventeen rubles to the dollar."

"Impossible," he said. "You would ruin me." We walked a few more yards. "Fourteen rubles."

"No," I said. I waited while we walked farther. "Sixteen."

"What do you think I am, a capitalist?" he demanded indignantly. "I will give you fifteen. No more."

There was a finality in his voice, and I knew that was about the right price. "All right," I said. "Where do we finish our business?"

The street ahead of us was deserted. He looked around and so did I. There were only the five youths. "Right here," he said.

I pulled out the money and counted off five hundred dollars without giving him a chance to see how much more I had. I passed it over to him. Without stopping, he held the money up so he could examine each bill yet he held it in a way so that no one would have known what he had unless they were very near. He grunted with satisfaction as he looked at each bill.

"It is good," he said finally. The money vanished somewhere in his clothes. He must have managed to count in his pocket, for he brought out a wad of ruble notes and handed them to me. I counted them, and there were exactly 7,500 rubles.

"You have more dollars?" he asked. He knew damn well I did, although he didn't know how many.

"Yes," I said. "I'll come back and see you when I want to sell them. Are you always in front of that restaurant?"

"Or inside. But only at night."

"I'll see you," I told him. I turned abruptly and went back to the five youths, who were maybe fifty feet behind us. I handed one of them a ten-dollar bill and kept on going. I knew that there was still a possibility that they might decide to follow and try to rob me, but I didn't look back. I cut off at the first intersection and didn't check until I reached Gorky Street again. There was no one behind me.

I went back to the hotel and up to my room. I got another one of the jazz records I had bought in Paris and wrapped it loosely in a sheet of paper from *Pravda*. I went back downstairs and asked directions to the Kotelnicheskaya Embankment. It wasn't far away and I walked. It had been roughly about forty minutes since I'd made the phone call, and I hoped that Zoya Aristova was still in her apartment.

The address turned out to be a fairly modern apartment building, with all sorts of stores on the ground floor, not unlike some of the big projects in New York. I soon found block G and entrance F. I prowled around inside, through halls heavy with the scents of cooking, until I found number 17. There was a light showing under the door, so she was probably home, unless she shared the apartment. But since she was a member of the KGB, I thought the chances were good that she had a place to herself.

I soon found a place, where the corridor branched off, that would enable me to keep a watch on her door without her seeing me if she came out. Then I had to hope that she would come out. If she turned out to be a homebody, I'd have to think of another approach. And maybe there wouldn't be time for that.

Time was the big problem, I thought as I leaned against the wall and settled down to wait. I'd now been in Moscow for about an hour and a half. There was no way to know for sure what Serov would do, but it was fairly logical to assume that he would stay in East Berlin until everyone was shipped out. I didn't know how many flights they needed, but it was probably a pretty big operation. It ought to give me a four- or five-hour edge, possibly more. An hour and a half was gone; that meant that Serov would be in Moscow in something over two and a half hours.

The trouble with this job was that there were too many unknown factors. If the girl was one of the agents who reported only to Serov, she certainly would still have the paper. She might or might not have left word for Serov to reach her the minute he returned to Moscow. My theory was that she would have done this—it was also safer to think that way. But she must know that she had gotten her hands on something important. So it seemed to me that was what she would do. On the other hand, Serov was an important enough man that he might not even check in at the KGB office until morning. Then again, he may have received the message in Berlin.

That's the way it went for the next hour while I waited. I went over and over all the possibilities and they all boiled down to one thing—I had very little time.

I had been waiting slightly more than an hour when her door opened. I drew back so that I could barely see down her corridor. She came into view, closing the door behind her. I had a brief glimpse of a short, dark-haired, pretty girl; then she headed down the corridor toward me and I had to pull back out of sight.

I had to be guided by the tap of her heels on the floor as she came down the corridor. When I judged that she was about to appear, I stepped briskly forward with my head down and not looking. It was good timing. I crashed right into her, hard enough to knock the breath out of her. The package beneath my arm slipped to the floor and I made certain that my foot smashed down on it. The paper flopped open so that the broken pieces of the record were clearly visible.

"*Izvinite!*" I exclaimed. "I'm terribly sorry. I'm afraid I wasn't looking where I was going."

"I'm afraid you weren't," she said with a smile. She glanced down at the broken record. "Oh, you broke your record. Was it something important?"

"It was an American recording of 'Muskrat Ramble,' " I said dolefully.

"Oh," she said with interest. "Wherever did you manage to get it?"

"In East Berlin," I said. "I was able to buy several records there. I am from Azerbaijan and I know only one person in Moscow. I came here tonight hoping to see him, and bring him the record as a present, but he wasn't home."

"That's too bad," she said. She was looking at me appraisingly. "Why are you in Moscow?"

"I'm a delegate to the trade conference."

"Oh, that's why you were in East Berlin," she said. She glanced at the record again. "I'm sorry that you broke your record."

"It's all right," I said. "At least it enabled me to meet a beautiful girl—even if only for a moment. But I am probably holding you up chattering away like this. You are probably on your way to a date with your young man."

"No," she said with another smile. "I was just going to have dinner by myself."

"Oh," I said. It had been a long time since I'd done the shy young man bit, but I tried. "I don't suppose—you wouldn't think of having dinner with me, would you?"

She hesitated only a minute. "I'd love to," she said. "After all, it is our socialistic duty to try to help comrades from out of the city."

We started walking down the corridor. "I am Mikhail Kirilenko," I said.

"Zoya Aristova," she answered.

"Rad poznakomitsya," I said. "I'm afraid that I am not yet familiar with Moscow. I arrived only a couple of hours ago. So the only place I know to suggest for dinner is my hotel."

"Where are you staying?"

"The National."

"Their food is good," she said. "I was thinking of going to the Praga, if you'd like to try another place."

"Fine."

"It is not cheap," she said. "But I can pay my share."

"No. I insist that you be my guest. I can afford it."

"All right," she said.

We took a taxi to the Praga. I already knew vaguely that it was one of Moscow's better restaurants, but I had never seen it, of course. It turned out to be very nice, and even the waiters seemed a little more attentive than the usual for Russia.

We both had several vodkas before we ordered dinner. We had caviar, *solyanka* soup, Wiener Schnitzel, semolina kasha with fruit, and black coffee.

We talked and became acquainted while we ate. One corner of the room was taken up with a bunch of boys and girls who wore imitation Western clothes.

"*Mitrofanushka,*"* Zoya said scornfully, pointing to them. "*Stilyagi.* They try to look like the stupid Americans and only succeed in looking foolish. They will one day find themselves in prison."

"They should," I said with a show of indignation. "Do they come here often?"

"All the time. They probably get the money by selling things in the black market."

"What about those over there?" I asked, pointing to another group of youths at a table across the room. They didn't look like the others, yet there was something different about them.

"*Nibonicho,*" she said. "The nonbelievers. Their slogan is *ni bogna, ni chorta,* 'neither God nor the Devil.' But they

---

* Mitrofan is the name of a good-for-nothing youth in a satirical Russian drama of the 18th century. The character's pet name, Mitrofanushka, became a nickname for an uneducated young man who lives off his well-to-do parents.

believe in nothing and they think this is a sign of intelligence."

"We have none of them in Azerbaijan," I said.

She smiled at me. "I think they exist only in Moscow. And there are not too many of them. You mustn't feel too righteous. You, too, like American things."

"I do not," I denied stoutly.

"What about jazz? Like the record you broke when you ran into me."

"That is different. The American jazz is a genuine folk music. It is not a product of their decadent capitalism."

"Don't be upset," she said. "I also like the American jazz. But it is difficult to get much of it here unless you're willing to buy it on the black market, and I wouldn't do that."

"Of course," I agreed, and signaled for the waiter.

The check when it came was the equivalent of about fifty dollars. I paid it and left a tip for the waiter even though there were signs that said tipping was forbidden. I saw by the expression on the waiter's face that I had done right.

We walked out of the restaurant. "Do you have a record player?" I asked her.

"Yes," she said. "But I do not have many records, especially jazz. I have others in Paris, where I work with our Embassy."

"I wonder," I said, getting shy again, "if we could perhaps play the records I brought from Berlin? I bought them to take home, but I would like to share them with you."

She hesitated again. "I would like that," she said finally, "but I should tell you that I may get a telephone call and have to go out even while we're playing the records. It will be business."

"All right," I said.

"Then we will do it," she said. She put her hand in mine. "Let us go, Mikhail."

We walked down the street, cutting over to Manezhnaya Square and on to the Hotel National. She waited in the lobby while I went upstairs and got the records I had brought with me. I also picked up the bottle of tablets that Henri had secured for me and put them in my pocket. I went back downstairs.

We took a taxi back to the Kotelnicheskaya Embankment. I stopped in one of the stores and bought a bottle of Stolichny vodka, then we went on to her apartment. It was similar to a one and a half room apartment in New York City. She had fixed it up very comfortably. We made drinks and started playing the records. I had made good choices. I had pressings of "The Empty Bed Blues," "There'll Be Some Changes Made," "Sugar Blue," "Rockin' Chair," "Really the Blues," "Jazz Me Blues," "Mandy," "Dippermouth," and many others. I was lucky that I had found a few she had never heard before.

Finally, after we'd had several drinks, I fixed fresh ones and slipped a tablet into her glass. I mixed the drink until I was sure the tablet was dissolved. Then I carried them over to where we sat near the record player. As I handed her the glass, I leaned over and kissed her lightly on the lips. She returned the pressure with her lips. I put another record on the player and sat next to her.

It took about twenty minutes after she finished her drink for the pill to go to work. She leaned against me and put her head on my shoulder. I could see her eyelids were getting heavy as we continued to listen to the music. I reached over and turned the volume down slightly.

Her head soon drooped against my shoulder and she began to snore softly. I waited a few more minutes, then eased her to the floor. Just to make sure, I lifted one of her eyelids and looked at her eye. She was out, all right.

Then I started searching the apartment. It wasn't very large, but there were still a lot of places to look. When I didn't find the paper in the more obvious places, I started looking everywhere. Under the carpet, behind the pictures, inside of pots. There wasn't a spot in the whole apartment that I missed, but I didn't find anything even vaguely resembling the paper I wanted. After about an hour I ended up empty-handed, standing over her inert body.

The only thing I'd missed was her purse, which was on the floor beside her. I picked it up and went through it. No paper. But I got curious about other things. She had a card identifying her as a member of the Russian Embassy in France. I took it from its case and examined it. Sure enough, it was a double card and I soon managed to pry off the thin card on the back of it. Anyway, we'd been right. It identified her, with picture and fingerprints, as a member of the KGB. It also gave her code name as Rozenka.

For a minute I wondered why that code name was familiar and then I remembered it was the one that Farley had mentioned in Berlin. The agent who was causing so much trouble in Europe who was known only as The Rose. Well, if I got away, this would at least end her usefulness.

The telephone started ringing. It sounded unpleasantly loud in the small apartment, but I was aware of the fact that it seemed that way partly because I was sure it was Serov, the head of the KGB, calling.

SIX

My time was even shorter. If that was Serov and the phone wasn't answered when he knew there was supposed to be an agent there waiting for his call, then he would probably have another agent at the door as quickly as he could get one. And that would be pretty quick.

And I still hadn't found the paper. That could mean that she had already given it to someone else or that it was merely hidden someplace I hadn't thought of looking.

While I was mulling it over, I was moving into action. I started to pick up Zoya so I could put her on the bed. She might be aware that she'd been drugged, in which case she'd know I'd done it. But if she didn't realize it, then she might not have any suspicions of me if I handled everything as normally as possible.

She was heavier than she looked, and I got a firmer grip, with my arm under her head and my hand in beneath her arm. My hand was touching her breast, and as her weight settled into my arms I felt something crackle slightly beneath my fingers.

I put her on the bed and quickly unbuttoned her blouse. I opened it and felt her brassiere. There was no doubt but what there was paper inside one cup. I felt the other one and there was no paper in it. I stripped off her blouse, unhooked her bra, and slipped it from her body. I had a small knife in my pocket and I used it to slit a few threads in the seam around the cup. It made enough of an opening for me to slip the piece of paper out. I unfolded it and looked at it. There was no mistake. This was what I was looking for. I didn't know the code, but it was obvious that it was a list of some sort and there was a CIA stamp on it.

I looked down at Zoya. She was pretty, with a slight flush on her face, her full breasts rising and falling as she breathed. But there was no time to admire her. I looked around the room until I found a piece of blank paper. I folded it and slipped it back into the opening in the cup of her brassiere. Then, with a little struggle, I got the bra back on her. I hooked it up and put on her blouse, buttoning it carefully.

I took a towel from her bathroom and went quickly over the room rubbing everything I thought I had touched. The MVD, and maybe the KGB, had my fingerprints, and I didn't want them finding out too quickly who I was. Then I collected my records.

I put the towel back and went to the door. I glanced down at the sleeping girl. "Sorry, honey," I said softly, "but that's the way it goes." I used the edge of my coat to turn the doorknob and stepped out into the hall. I closed the door gently and left the building. I walked back to my hotel. That way there'd be no taxi driver to report what time I left.

Buying a bottle of vodka at the hotel, I went up to my room. I poured myself a stiff drink and sat down to think over the next step. I was certain that I had the paper I'd come for; the next thing was to make sure that I got away with it with the least amount of trouble. My problem was to find the best way of doing it. I still had to convert most of my dollars into rubles. And there was another angle. If Mikhail Kirilenko vanished the same night he arrived in Moscow, it might attract more attention than if he disappeared later. But if he waited too long to vanish, that might be the end of Milo March, too.

I dug the program of events out of Mikhail's suitcase and looked at it. The only thing scheduled for the next day was a luncheon at which the delegates would be greeted by Premier Khrushchev. I noticed, however, that it wasn't an invitation; it directed the delegates to be there. If Mikhail Kirilenko was absent at the reception, it might start an immediate search. If he showed up, it might mean the arrest of Milo March.

But would it? That was the big question. All I could do was try to guess what would happen. It was true that when Serov failed to get an answer to his phone call—if that had been him calling—he might send another agent around to the apartment. But I doubted that the other agent would force an entrance if he got no answer at the door. There would be no reason for them to suspect that something had actually happened to her right in the heart of Moscow. So, I thought, it would be logical for Serov to think she'd gone out for the evening and that she would report the following morning.

Zoya would sleep through the night, all right. I'd given her enough drug to make sure of that. In fact, it should be almost noon before she came out of it. After that, it would be a gamble. Being an agent, she probably would be suspicious of the reason she had passed out. Her first reaction would be to see if she still had the paper. If she merely felt at her brassiere and was reassured by the feel of the paper there, then her suspicions might fade and I'd be safe until she went to turn the paper over to Serov. When that happened, it would certainly be all over with Mikhail Kirilenko. From then on it would just be Milo March on the run.

I took another look at the program for the luncheon. The delegates were promised a generous showing of Russian celebrities. Headed by Khrushchev, we were supposed to be greeted by Mikoyan, Kirichenko, Furtseva, Voroshilov, Bulganin, Kozlov, and Mukhitdinov, all members of the Presidium of the Central Committee of the Communist Party. And General Ivan Alexandrovich Serov and Nikolai Pavlovich Dudorov, the heads of the KGB and the MVD.

So Serov was to be at the luncheon, too. That meant if Zoya didn't reach him before he went to the luncheon, she might not find out that the paper was gone until late in the afternoon. The problem was, could I afford to take that gamble?

It was already close to midnight. Even if I could get my dollars changed to rubles at once, it might be difficult to try to leave right away. I knew that traveling late at night might be dangerous, since it was unusual enough in the Soviet Union to attract a lot of attention. I'd probably have to stay over until morning no matter what happened. So I'd be gambling on staying around an extra five or six hours, and if I got away with it, there might be advantages.

Finally I faced the fact that I was kidding myself. The truth of the matter was, I wanted to go to that luncheon. I liked the idea of an American agent being able to walk into the Kremlin and have a few drinks with Khrushchev and his pack. I might never get another chance. Of course, all of this was merely another part of working as an agent. It gets into your blood and after a while you keep wondering what you can get away with next. Then you start taking chances, and quite often that's the end of another agent.

But once I'd faced the fact that I wanted to go to the party, I felt better. I'd go and take my chances. General Roberts would blow his top if he knew about it, but I might as well have some fun out of it.

I had another quick drink of vodka and left the hotel. It didn't take me long to get back to the restaurant where I'd met the black market operator earlier in the evening. He was still in front of the restaurant. There was no one else around, although there were still quite a few people strolling around on the street. Nearly all of them were young.

"I want to talk to you," I told him as I stopped in front of him.

"All right," Nuritdin said. "We will take a walk."

"Why?" I asked. "Can't we go inside and talk over coffee?"

"Not wise," he grunted. "There are still customers in there. Who knows who they are?"

"Who knows who I am?" I retorted. "Well, if we can't go inside, why can't we just stand here and talk? There's no one to overhear."

He shook his head. "We will walk."

"I still want to know why," I said as we started down the street. I was curious about it suddenly, for I realized that I hadn't seen anyone standing around on the streets anywhere in Moscow as you would in almost any other city in the world.

"You are a stranger?" he asked. I couldn't tell whether he sounded suspicious or not.

"In Moscow," I said. "I come from the south, where people often stand on the street."

"Then you are foolish. In Moscow, to stand on the street is *nekrasivo.* Improper. Besides, the police get more interested in those who are standing idly than in those who seem to be going somewhere."

"Oh," I said. That made sense. "I want to sell more dollars and I want to sell them quickly."

"How much?"

"Eight thousand dollars." I'd decided that I'd keep fifteen hundred in dollars. I'd have to go through another country when I left Russia, and I might need dollars there because I probably wouldn't be able to use rubles.

"You think I carry a hundred and twenty thousand rubles around in my pocket like so many tobacco crumbs?" he asked scornfully.

"No," I said, "but I think you could do something about it if you wanted to get dollars."

"I'll have to share it with someone else," he grumbled. "I cannot buy that many dollars myself."

"So share it with someone else or I will go elsewhere," I said.

"All right, all right," he said. We walked on in silence for another block. Then we came to a small café that was still open. "Go in here and wait," he said. "This place stays open later than most restaurants because there are night workers near here who come in after one."

"How long?" I asked.

"Perhaps a half hour," he said. "Perhaps longer. I cannot tell exactly. But I will come back."

"All right," I said. "But hurry, for I will not wait all night." I went into the café. There were only six or seven people there at the moment. I found a small table in the corner and sat down. After about five minutes an old waiter shuffled over and stood looking at me. I ordered *sosiski,* which are boiled frankfurters, and a bottle of beer.

Fifteen minutes later he came back and plumped the dish of frankfurters, the bottle of beer, and a glass down in front of me. "Twelve rubles," he said.

I gave him fifteen rubles and told him to keep the change. He looked slightly more pleasant about the transaction but that was all.

I was on my third bottle of beer before Nuritdin showed up. He slipped into the chair opposite me and stared glumly across the table.

"All right," he said.

"Good," I said. "Will you have a glass of beer?"

He hesitated, then nodded. "Yes, but there must be no talking of business while we are here."

I gestured, and the waiter, who was now practically an old friend, hurried over. I told him to bring another bottle of beer. He went back and soon returned with it. I paid him and added another tip.

"I do not like to be seen with you," Nuritdin grumbled. "You look too prosperous. It may make someone suspicious of me."

"I'm an important man," I said gravely. "Is there anything wrong with the fact that I want to become acquainted with my comrades in Moscow?"

"Important people do not become acquainted with me." He gulped his beer. "But many of them do business with me," he added almost viciously.

We finished our beer in silence and then left the restaurant. Again we walked along the street. Now there were few people on it. Even so, he was careful to wait until there was no one in sight.

"You have the dollars?" he asked.

I produced the eight thousand dollars, which I had already separated from the rest of my dollars. He counted them quickly and secretively.

"Khorosho," he said. He dug into his clothing and produced a great wad of ruble notes. He handed them to me.

I stopped for a minute beneath a streetlight, even though it made him nervous, and did a quick count. It was the right amount.

"Fine," I said. "Now I want to know something else."

"What?"

"Where in Moscow, now, tonight, can I rent a room? It must be mine alone with a private entrance so that my going or coming will not be watched. And it must not be reported to the police that it has been rented to me."

"Do you think this is Paris?" he asked sarcastically. "It is hard enough to find a place to live in Moscow without all the things you also demand."

"When things are being sold on the street," I said, "then

everything is for sale. For a price. Was it not the great Dostoevski himself who wrote that man is a pliable animal who gets accustomed to everything?"

"True," he said glumly. "It would be expensive."

"It is understood," I said dryly, "that anything purchased through you will be expensive."

He gave me a glance without actually looking directly at me. "Why do you need such a place? Do you have no place to stay?"

"I have a very fine hotel room. But let us suppose a situation. It is agreed that we Russians are passionate people. So suppose that I wish to enjoy a few moments of romance with the wife of an important man here in Moscow. Can I take her to my hotel? Can I take her to an apartment which is shared with others who will have long tongues? Would you have me commit suicide?"

"Ah," he said understandingly. "But I cannot imagine that one would want to be alone with the wives of most important men. Their mistresses, perhaps ..."

"This is not the wife of most of the men," I said shortly. "It is wife of only one. And the rental price of the room does not include your approval."

"How long would you want it?"

"No more than two or three days. And nights. But I will pay for at least four days in advance."

"Perhaps it could be done," he said. "But it would be expensive. Perhaps as much as three hundred rubles the night." He wasn't joking about its being expensive. At the official rate that was thirty dollars a night, and I could already imagine that it wouldn't be much of a room. But I might need it a lot more than I would need the money.

"All right," I said. "And I'll pay for four days, as I said. But it must be understood that if anything gets out about this, I will naturally talk about the dollars that I sold. And I have the numbers that were on the bills."

"You wound me," he said, but without much feeling. He lived in a world that expected everyone to be suspicious of everyone else. "This is a transaction of sentiment, and one does not talk about such things."

Some sentiment, at thirty dollars per day. But I thought he would keep his mouth shut, not because of sentiment but because it would be good business.

"All right," I said. "Take me to it."

"You want it starting tonight?"

"Starting tonight."

He sighed, but turned at the next block and led the way. We walked about ten blocks and ended up at an apartment house that looked as if it might have been on the Lower East Side in New York. He led the way up a back stairway and finally stopped on the third floor and knocked on a door. I stayed a few feet away while he had a low-voiced conversation with whoever answered the door. Then he came back to where I stood.

"It is arranged," he said. "They will be out within a few minutes. If you have paid the money."

I took the hint. I pulled the money from my pocket and counted out twelve hundred rubles. "It is understood," I said, "that no one will try to use it or even come around while I have it?"

"It is understood," he said.

I thought he was probably turning his own family, or at least some relative, out and that they would probably have to move in with some other family who already lived in crowded quarters, and I felt bad about it for a moment. But I eased my feelings by thinking that they were getting enough money out of it to make other things a little easier for them.

"There is only one key," he said, "so you can be sure no one can enter."

"What do I do with it when I leave?" I asked.

"Place it beneath the garbage can by the door," he said.

We waited about ten or fifteen minutes and then two women, a man, and two children came out. Nuritdin talked to them for another minute and then came over to hand me a key. Then they all left. I waited until they had gone down the stairs before I went in.

It was a one-room apartment, but it was quite a different thing from the one I'd been in earlier. There was a blanket stretched across the room so that it could be turned into two sections. There was a bed in each side, and two beds had been made up on the floor for the children. In one corner there was a sink and a small stove. The windows were taped and the air was stale. A frayed clothesline stretched across one end of the room.

After I had checked over the room, I left, locking the door behind me. I went downstairs and checked carefully so that I knew I would have no trouble finding the place again. Then I set out for the hotel. It was a good walk from there, but I decided it was better to go on foot than to try to find a taxi at that hour. There were very few people on the streets, but nothing happened during the walk back. It did seem to me that the MVD man on duty in front of the Hotel National looked at me somewhat suspiciously, but it may have been my imagination.

I went straight up to my room. I relaxed with a large glass of vodka and then went to bed. It had been a hard enough day so that I went to sleep almost immediately.

I was awake fairly early the following morning. I rang a bell in the room and after a few minutes a waiter showed up. He brought me *vinogradnaya sok,* which was just plain grape juice, and a pot of coffee.

After breakfast I made myself as ready for what might follow as it was possible to do. I kept only a few things on myself. My money, the paper I'd taken from Zoya, the identification of Mikhail Kirilenko, one thin slip of paper that gave my own identification, the bottle of knockout pills, and a set of lock picks (the only things of my own that I'd brought from Berlin). I took a last drink from the bottle of vodka and left the hotel. I didn't want to hang around there until it was time for me to show up at the luncheon.

I walked down to the Moscow River where well-kept trees lined the water. I found a comfortable place to sit and stayed there, watching the streamlined river buses going back and forth. It was a peaceful spot and it was almost possible to forget that I was only a few hundred yards from one of the hot spots of the Cold War. But if I looked over my shoulder, I was reminded of reality by the sight of the mosque-like towers of the Kremlin buildings.

I stayed by the river until it was time to go to the luncheon. I got up and walked back to the street. Just before I reached the Kremlin, I stopped at a phone booth on the street. I deposited fifteen kopecks and called the Hotel National. When they answered, I asked for Mikhail Kirilenko. There was a short wait and then I was informed that he was out. That was all. But it made me feel better because I was sure there would have been an attempt to find out who was calling if the heat had been on. I replaced the phone receiver and walked on to the building where the luncheon was being held.

There was a generous squad of uniformed MVD men at the entrance and there were probably a few KGB men among them, but there was no way of knowing. One of the men looked at my identification with a bored expression, checked it against a list, and waved me inside.

The main room was huge. There were several long tables, all of them literally heaped with food. A large number of servants were circling among the guests, making sure that their glasses were never empty.

I was stopped at the entrance to the room by a polite official who wanted to know who I was. I showed him my identification and he fished around in a box in front of him and came up with a paper and cellophane badge with *Mikhail Kirilenko* and *Azerbaijan S.S.R.* on it. I pinned it to the lapel of my coat and went on in. Except for the language on the badge, it was almost like being at a convention of Rotarians back in the States.

A glass of vodka was shoved into my hand before I had taken more than ten steps into the room. Sipping it, I began to weave through the other guests, most of whom were gathered in various little knots busily talking. I had no way of being certain that Azerbaijan wouldn't have additional delegates to the Moscow convention even though they had sent only one to East Berlin, so I managed to hold my arm so as to partly conceal my badge. I kept circulating until I found a man standing by himself near the outer edge of the group. He was gulping vodka as though it were water and his cheeks were flushed enough to show that he was already getting stoned. A glance at his badge showed me that he was from the Belarusian Republic. That seemed far enough away from Azerbaijan to be safe. I stopped beside him.

"Quite a party," I said.

He glanced at me, then decided he didn't know me but that it was all right. He grinned, showing a row of stainless steel teeth. "Yes," he said. "That is because it's a Party party." He giggled as though to make sure that I understood it was a joke. I laughed politely and that seemed to make him feel better.

"None of the important visitors here yet?" I asked.

"I don't think so," he said. He glanced around. "I imagine they will be here soon. Have you heard the latest story in Moscow about Premier Khrushchev?"

"No," I admitted.

"It seems," he said, lowering his voice confidentially, "that the Premier went to the airport to meet some important comrades from China. While he was waiting for the plane to land, he noticed that his shoe was untied. He bent to tie it and his trousers split. In the seat. It was a terrible moment. He went quickly to the waiting room, thinking someone there might have a needle and thread. But as he entered, an attendant rushed up with a pair of pants. You can imagine how astonished the Premier was, and he wanted to know how the attendant knew that he needed a pair of pants. 'We just heard it,' the attendant said, 'on the Voice of America.' "

He roared with laughter and I joined in, although I wasn't sure that his type of humor was the safest.

"It is funny, no?" he exclaimed digging his elbow into my ribs. "You know who told me that joke? It was Premier Khrushchev himself. In East Berlin. Were you there?"

I told him that I had been but that I had been ill and was forced to miss the Premier's speech. He consoled me, telling me how much I had missed and bragging about the long conversation he'd had with Khrushchev.

I'd just decided that he was probably just making himself a big man, when I saw that Khrushchev and a group of men had entered the room. I recognized Mikoyan and Serov among those with him. They all immediately grabbed glasses of vodka and began to mingle with the guests.

"There is your friend now," I said. "Why don't you rush over and embrace him?"

He looked nervous and I knew I'd been right. "He's a very busy man," he mumbled. "I will see him later after he's been polite to everyone."

"That's a good idea," I agreed gravely. "By the way, one of the men with him is going to be looking for me, although he's never met me. How would you like to help me play a joke on him?"

His face brightened up. He was glad to get off the hook, but then he probably also liked the idea of practical jokes. "What do we do?" he asked.

"It is simple," I said. "We merely exchange badges, and when he comes up to you, he will think you are me. You can play along with whatever he says and later we will have a big laugh on him."

"It is an excellent joke," he said. He giggled drunkenly and unfastened the badge on his lapel. I took off my own and pinned it to his coat, then put his on my lapel.

"Don't tell anyone," I said, winking at him. "It would spoil the joke if he should learn about it."

"You may depend on me," he said. He took a full glass of vodka from a passing servant.

"Good," I said. "How are things in your republic?"

"Wonderful. Production everywhere is higher than it has ever been, especially in the Automobile and Tractor Works in Minsk. And we have a forty-eight-million-ruble clothing factory almost ready to begin production in Molodechno."

"You amaze me," I said. "Well, I will see you later and we will have a big laugh on my friend."

"You bet," he said. He flashed the stainless steel teeth again.

I turned and worked my way back through the crowd until I was fairly near to the Khrushchev party. They were nearly all drinking heavily, too, but it didn't seem to interfere with the very thorough political job they seemed to be doing with the delegates. Khrushchev especially was obviously being charming, and I could see that most of the delegates were being properly impressed. The only member of the group who didn't seem to be exerting himself was Serov. The head of the KGB looked preoccupied and kept glancing back at the entrance to the room.

I felt a little tingle of excitement and knew it came from the fact that my first impression was that Serov was waiting for information about Zoya Aristova. It was the kind of feeling that most people would ignore, but after you've been in the business as long as I have, you come to respect those feelings.

It was time for me to get out, but if I could stay long enough to find out what was going on, it might help. I looked around me. The room had three exits besides the way I had entered, although I didn't know where they led. Maybe I'd have a chance to find out. There was also a long row of windows along the far wall. The room was on the second floor, so they might offer a possibility if I did get cornered. There were no uniformed men in the room, but I was certain that there must be some KGB men there disguised as delegates. Perhaps not many, however, for it was said that Khrushchev had cut down on the number of men guarding him whenever he was among his own people.

My musing was stopped by Khrushchev looming up in front of me. His sharp little eyes glanced at my face and moved on to the badge on my lapel. "Ah, one of our White Russians," he said jovially. "Tell me, how does it go with that clothing mill we've been building in Molodechno?"

"Fine," I said nervously. I didn't have to put that on; just having him that near to me was enough to produce it. I struggled and remembered something that had been said by the man with whom I had changed badges. "It will soon be completed and then you will see the best production in the world. After all, it has cost forty-eight million rubles and it should be the best in the world."

"That's the spirit," he said. He made a fist and poked me lightly on the arm. "We will soon beat those Americans, eh?"

He moved on before I could answer, stopping by the next man. "A Moldavian comrade," I heard him say, but his voice didn't sound so cordial. "When are we going to start getting better cattle from your republic? All I hear are complaints."

The man mumbled some reply that I did not hear. It wasn't even important. I realized something then about Khrushchev. He probably had more power than any man in the world, but he was also a superb politician. He had barely looked at my face, but had been more interested in where I was from. He probably did know a great deal about every part of the Soviet Union and he automatically came up with something pertinent at the sight of a name. He was like the old-time ward heelers, only smarter and even more ruthless.

I was about to work my way out of the crowd, to go examine the exits, when I caught sight of a man hurrying into the room. He was dressed in a plain gray suit, but he still looked like a cop. His gaze swept around the room and stopped on Serov. At the same time, Serov saw him and nodded slightly. The man hurried across the room. I moved casually forward so that I would be nearer. By the time the two men came together I was no more than four or five feet away. I pretended to be interested in something that two delegates were saying to each other.

"We have her," the man said to Serov. He was keeping his

voice low but I could hear him. "She was in her apartment only partly awake. She had been drugged. We have proved that."

Serov said something that I did not hear.

"It is gone. She had it hidden in her clothing, but another paper has been substituted for it."

"How?" Serov asked. He bit the word off.

"She has confessed. She entertained a man last night. They were drinking and playing American jazz records the man had smuggled into the Soviet Union. There is no question that he drugged her when they were drinking and took the paper. She was unconscious all night and all morning."

"A man she knew?"

"She only met him last night. In the hallway of her building. It is obvious the man arranged to meet her there."

"She would know him if she saw him again?"

"Yes. But she also remembered the name he gave her."

"Who?"

"Mikhail Kirilenko. He is listed as the delegate to this meeting from Azerbaijan."

General Serov looked around and I became very active signaling a servant for a fresh glass of vodka. By the time it had arrived, they were talking together again.

"Bring in four or five men," Serov ordered. "That should be enough. Have them find him and take him out quietly."

"Yes, sir," the man said. "But that is not all."

"What?"

"We went over her room carefully. Someone had wiped off the bottle, glasses, and almost everything in the room. But we found fingerprints on the paper that was substituted for the one she was bringing us."

I cursed softly to myself.

"Yes?" Serov asked.

"They were the prints of the American agent, Milo March. So it is he who is here pretending to be the delegate from Azerbaijan."

SEVEN

I showed great interest in my glass of vodka as General Serov cursed. Russian is a very expressive language and he made full use of it.

"He came here today?" he asked finally.

"Someone came in under the name of Kirilenko. It is probably the American."

"Then we will get him this time. It will not be bungled as the MVD did three years ago in Berlin. Bring in ten men. If possible, make it quiet—but get him."

"Yes, sir. What about Aristova?"

"Keep her under arrest. We will try her with the American and execute them together."

"Yes, sir." The man turned and hurried out.

Well, I had a few minutes and not much more. I started to stroll past Serov. He glanced at me sharply, his gaze going to my badge. He read it and lost interest in me. He started walking toward the other delegates as I headed for the entrance. If I had a chance to get out now, it was only through the main exit. As I reached the doorway I began to stagger, splashing some of the vodka from the glass I carried. I could feel the tightness in the muscles of my stomach—and in a way it was a good feeling.

I was halfway down the corridor when I met the squad

of men coming in on the double. They were all in plain-clothes, but they all looked like cops. They had the corridor pretty well blocked, so I stopped and stared at them, grinning drunkenly and swaying slightly.

"You are late for the party, comrades," I said, slurring my words. "If that is the way you meet production schedules, it will not be good."

"Who are you?" barked the man who had been talking to Serov.

"Forget," I said foolishly. I pretended that I was trying to see the badge on my lapel. "Can't get lost, though. It tells right here."

He came closer and looked at the badge. Then he relaxed slightly. "Where are you going?" he asked.

"Need a little fresh air," I said. " 'S too warm in there." I breathed vodka fumes into his face.

"All right," he said, laughing. He nodded to his men and they strode purposefully past me. I staggered on my way down the stairs to the ground floor. I stood, swaying, for a minute in the doorway, blinking owlishly at the sunlight. Then I stepped out, aiming myself carefully for the space between the groups of uniformed MVD men. One of them stepped forward, glancing at the identification badge on my lapel.

"Where are you going, comrade?" he asked.

"Fresh air," I said indistinctly. "Very warm in there. Got to get fresh air and go back to drink a toast with Premier Khrushchev."

"All right, but don't go too far," he said. He reached out

and took the glass from my hand. "Better give me the glass, comrade, so that you don't get accused of stealing state property." He and the other MVD men laughed. One of them made a joke as I staggered away.

I walked down the street toward Manezhnaya Square, forcing myself to go slowly and aware of the prickling tension in the middle of my back. I reached the corner and turned. Two more steps and I was out of sight of the MVD men. I quickly removed the badge from my lapel and shoved it into my pocket. There was a taxi about a block away and I waved it down to me. I climbed in and gave him an address on Gorky Street that I knew would be about ten blocks away.

I sank back against the seat and drew my first relaxed breath as the cab took off. As we passed the entrance to the center of the Kremlin, I caught a brief glimpse of the plainclothesmen hustling a figure out of the building. My brief Belarusian friend was in for a rough time until they checked and discovered he was neither Milo March nor Mikhail Kirilenko. That ought to take an hour or so, but then he'd be all right.

The taxi stopped ten blocks away and I got out. I waited until it had driven out of sight, then I set out for the apartment I had rented the night before. It didn't take me too long to get oriented, and then I walked to it within a few minutes. On the way, I tore Mikhail Kirilenko's identification and the Belarusian badge to small bits and scattered them a piece at a time.

Just before I reached the apartment I stopped and bought of bottle of vodka. I went up to the apartment, poured myself a drink, lit a cigarette, and then sat there grinning at myself. I had cut it a little too fine, but I'd made out all right so far.

Only one thing bothered me. I kept seeing Zoya Aristova as I'd seen her lying on the bed, her blouse off, her black hair billowing around a face relaxed in sleep, and then thinking of her in prison and what was ahead of her. Maybe it was silly; she was an agent and could be expected to take the same risks I did. But agents also get to thinking of other agents as different from other people. Up to this moment Zoya Aristova had been merely someone to defeat, almost as unemotional as a chess problem, but now that I had gotten what I came after, I was thinking of her as a human being.

There would probably be no escape for her. The value of the CIA paper must have been built up in advance, and then she had let an American agent walk into the heart of Moscow and take it back. Serov would not be inclined to be lenient about that. He had been a deputy commissar of the old NKVD, then a deputy minister of MVD; he'd been trained by Beria,* even though he hadn't been close enough to fall with him, so he was not apt to forgive even the slightest transgression. She'd be lucky if execution was all that happened to her.

I had a couple more drinks of vodka and by that time I had made up my mind. I stretched out on one of the beds and went to sleep.

It was early evening when I awakened, within a few minutes of the time I'd decided to get up. I went to the sink and washed my face in cold water. I had a shot of vodka for an eye opener, then left. I walked the few blocks to the restaurant

---

* Laventry Beria was head of security and secret police under Stalin. At that time the organization was called the NKVD (Narodnyi Komissariat Vnutrennikh Del, People's Commissariat for Internal Affairs); later it became the KGB. His downfall came in 1953, when he was arrested and executed for treason.

where Nuritdin hung out. He was already there. His expression, as he saw me, was mixed.

"Dobre vecher," he said, but there wasn't much enthusiasm in his voice.

"Good evening," I replied. "Can we take a walk?"

He nodded glumly and we started down the street. "You disturb me," he complained. "I have customers who come to see me once a week, once every two weeks—but you came around twice a day. It is not natural. Are you standing with your hand in Khrushchev's pocket that you have so much to sell? Who are you? I do not see your picture in *Pravda*. How do you come by so many dollars? Are you the President of America? What do you wish to sell this time?"

I grinned at him. "I'm the American ambassador to the black market," I said. "A member of the vicuña-coat diplomacy.* But this time I don't want to sell; I want to buy."

He looked at me suspiciously. "What?"

"Many things. First, I'd like to buy a car."

"On the black market?"

I nodded.

"It can be done," he admitted. "You can get a Pobeda for forty thousand rubles. You can have it in two or three days."

I had at least seen pictures of the Pobeda. It was a small car that looked something like an American Chevrolet of 1950.

---

* The vicuña coat is a symbol of bribery. In a scandal of the Eisenhower administration, a vicuña coat was one of the expensive gifts given to the White House Chief of Staff, Sherman Adams, by an industrialist who was under investigation by the FTC. Adams resigned in 1958 after he was accused of doing favors for the industrialist. In 1959, Premier Khrushchev's Italian tailor made a vicuña coat as a gift for President Eisenhower. He claimed he knew nothing about Sherman Adams before he announced his plan to present the gift.

Forty thousand rubles would make it cost about four thousand dollars.

"Too much money," I said. "I won't pay that much. And I have to have it tonight, not in two or three days."

"That's the trouble with you," he grumbled. "You are not from Moscow yet you know too much. It is disturbing."

"Do I get the car and for a decent price?" I asked.

He sighed. "Thirty thousand rubles. And you can have the car in five hours."

"Where?"

"The street behind the restaurant."

"Good."

"Payment in advance," he said.

"No," I said. "I'll give you a thousand rubles now and twenty-nine thousand rubles when the car is delivered. And it has to be a new one. I won't accept any old car that you feel free to steal off the streets so that I'll be picked up ten minutes after I drive away in it."

"All right," he said. He glanced at me out of the corners of his eyes. "You worry me, comrade. You are too smart. All of my customers drive hard bargains, but they are not smart. ... Give me the money."

I counted out a thousand rubles and passed it to him. "I want to buy something else," I said, "but first I want some information and I don't intend to pay for it. You know about the KGB?"

"*Oni!*" he exclaimed. "Who does not know about the secret police? It is possible to live and not know about them?"

"Here in Moscow," I said, "if the KGB arrested one of their own, where would they keep him?"

"Is that part of your romance?" he asked sarcastically.

"It could be," I said cheerfully. "Where?"

"The Uzbekistan Prison. It is at the end of Kuznetsky Most, just below the Kremlin. It is the prison reserved for those in the MVD and KGB who defect in any way. It is said to be a terrible place."

"I'm sure of it," I said. "I want to buy two things. First, I want a plan of the Uzbekistan Prison and I want it within two hours. How much will it cost?"

"Would you also like a key to the prison?" he asked dryly.

"I don't need it. What about the plan?"

He was silent while we walked a hundred feet. "It is possible," he said finally. "But it will have to be drawn from memory, and it will be expensive. Such things are dangerous, you know."

"Nonsense," I said. "In the first place, I will merely examine the drawing and then, in your presence, I will burn it. So you can see there will be nothing to be dangerous. How much?"

"A thousand rubles," he said with resignation.

It was too much, but it wasn't high enough to argue about. "All right," I said. "In two hours?"

"In two hours."

"The second thing I want," I said, "is identification papers. For two people. A man and a woman. They must be papers that will enable us to travel from one republic to another and they must be well made. What about it?"

"That is more difficult," he began.

"I know," I said. "Anything to push the price up. This is understood. Let us not waste time with these foolish things. Tell me how much and how long."

"You are difficult, comrade," he complained. "Such a thing as you ask is not possible in less than two days, and it will be expensive. It requires fine workmanship to fool the police, and even then it cannot be guaranteed."

"How much?"

"Ten thousand rubles."

"I'll tell you what I'll do," I said. "I want the papers inside of five hours. I don't care what names are on them. Any names as long as they fit a man and woman. You can use me for the model of the man and the girl is about twenty-five, five feet four, one hundred and twenty pounds, black hair. If I can have them in five hours, I'll pay twenty thousand rubles. Longer than five hours and the whole deal is off."

"More romance?" he asked with sarcasm.

"Why not?" I responded. "The lady and I both like to travel, and it would not be wise to travel under our own names. It's not just a question of our personal safety. Think what it would do if the capitalistic press in other countries discovered us. You will be performing a patriotic duty to Mother Russia as well as making a nice socialistic profit."

"You use words too well, comrade," he said. "I do not trust it. But don't worry. I will ask no questions. I have a feeling that it is not safe to ask questions of you. I do not want to know what you do. I can't even afford to do business with you."

"You can't afford not to do business with me," I said gently. "Remember that I still have the numbers on the dollars that I sold to you."

"I remember," he said sadly. "How could I forget, comrade?

You will not permit it. I do not understand you. I do not want to."

"That's good. Well?"

"I cannot guarantee the delivery. I will see if it can be obtained in five hours, but I do not know it it's possible."

"You try. I'm sure it can be done. For twenty thousand rubles. But in five hours. With the car."

He nodded. "In all, comrade, you are asking me to deliver things worth fifty-one thousand rubles, and I have only one thousand rubles in my pocket. You are asking much."

"I will give you one thousand rubles more on account," I told him. "But that's all. You deliver everything and you will get the remaining forty-nine thousand. That's the way it has to be."

"All right."

I counted out another thousand rubles and gave them to him. "I will see you in front of the restaurant in two hours," I said.

Nuritdin nodded and we parted company. I walked on down the street alone while he went back the way we had come. I had two hours to kill and I had no identification at all—except the thin slip of paper which showed that I was Milo March, U.S.A. Major. The problem was to spend that two hours where I couldn't be asked about who I was, since I was sure there was already a search on for me.

I finally hit on an idea. I stopped at the first theater I came to. It was a play, *The Bedbug* by Mayakovski. I went in, checking my coat and renting a pair of opera glasses. I didn't think I'd need them, but I knew that the possession of them would help me get my coat out of check later without waiting in line.

The play wasn't the greatest, but it wasn't too bad. I had to leave a few minutes before the final curtain. Nobody paid any attention to me as I sneaked out, but the check girl did give me a disapproving look as I turned in the opera glasses and received my coat. I went out and headed for the restaurant. I was there within ten minutes.

Nuritdin was standing in front as usual. He nodded as I came up and immediately started down the street. I fell into step with him. We walked a block before he said anything.

"I have the plan," he said then. "That was to be a thousand rubles."

I counted out a thousand rubles and passed them over to him. He handed me back a single sheet of paper. I glanced at it as we walked along the street. It was a crude but effective drawing of the two floors of a prison. The layout was a simple one, but complete, including the location of the guards' office near the entrance, and I quickly memorized it. I pulled a package of matches from my pocket, struck one, and held it to the paper. It caught fire and burned quickly. The last flaming piece floated from my fingers to the ground.

"Satisfied?" I asked.

"*Da,*" he grunted.

"You have three more hours on the other things," I said. "How is it going?"

"The car will be there," he said. "Perhaps the papers. I do not know."

"All right," I said. "I will see you in three hours." He nodded and turned back down the street. I went ahead, cutting over to Gorky Street. I walked along, keeping a careful watch. I knew what I wanted in a rough way and I didn't intend to plan it any more carefully than that. It always went better if the outline was not too complete.

I kept stopping and looking into every restaurant and bar that I came to. Several times I saw uniformed MVD men drinking or eating, but they didn't interest me. Finally, I cut across in a different direction. When I reached Tchaikovsky Street, I turned down it. I walked along for several blocks without spotting a single restaurant or bar. Finally, I saw ahead of me a building with a familiar object projecting in front of it. The American flag. It was the United States Embassy.

I grinned to myself at the irony of it. I hadn't planned on going near it, but here I was only a few yards from the one spot in Russia that was American property. I could easily walk inside and have nothing to worry about as long as I stayed there, but I couldn't do it. Even if it had been a normal situation, I couldn't have gone there; it was part of the rules that you couldn't openly involve your own government. But now it was worse. I'd heard enough to know that they had identified me. The Soviet government would try—maybe had already started—to use it as a propaganda weapon. They would claim that an American agent named Milo March was in Russian territory. It would be officially denied in Washington. And with honesty, because no one knew that I was there except the four men who had been in that hotel suite just a few nights earlier. If I went to the Embassy I would get protection, but the damage would be untold. So I merely gave the building a small salute in my heart and forgot about it.

Almost. The part of not forgetting had to do with something else. When I was still fifty yards away from the building, I saw a uniformed man approaching the front of it. He greeted another uniformed man and the second one left. I realized what it was. The changing of the guard. There was an MVD man in the front of every public building in Moscow. The American Embassy was no exception. It was merely time for a change of shift. But the man who had just left looked just about right. I quickened my pace so I would be a little nearer him. He marched rather proudly in his blue coat with its red and white tabs, and since he was then off duty, I guessed he was probably new. But I also noticed, as he passed beneath a streetlight, that he was a sergeant. I would have preferred a higher rank, but I could no longer be so particular.

He went about four blocks and finally turned into a small café. I followed him inside and took a table next to his. He had already ordered a beer. I ordered a hundred grams of vodka. I ignored him until after we had been drinking a few minutes.

"Prastiti," I said. "I was walking down the street behind you and I could not help but notice that you were on duty in front of the American Embassy."

"Yes," he said, but with a friendly smile.

"Is it true," I asked, "that there are spies going in and out of there all the time?"

"It could be," he said solemnly. "There are many persons who go in there, and I can assure you that they look very strange, but it is not up to me to say what they are. I stay there during my duty and report what happens and that is all."

"Very proper," I said solemnly. "But it is too bad that we must be threatened by these enemies in our midst."

"True," he said. "But it is not to worry. Premier Khrushchev has said that we will soon defeat the Americans in the production of goods."

"It is true," I said. "It is I who should know it. I am a trades representative. From Riga." I gave myself the first Russian name I could think of. "Bielov."

"Sergeiev," he said, giving his own name in return. We continued to talk, and after a few minutes I succeeded in buying him a vodka. After that it was somewhat easier and I bought him several vodkas. I learned that he was single and lived with his mother and three brothers and one sister in a two-room apartment. After he had gotten a little tipsy I gave him a story about the two girls I was supposed to meet later in the apartment I was living in. I waited for a half hour, and two more vodkas, before I suggested that he might come along. By that time he was so interested he almost fell on his face nodding his head. I paid the bill and we left the restaurant.

We walked across town. It was still early and there were a lot of people on the street. I noticed that most of them got very interested in something else the minute they saw the MVD uniform. We finally reached the building where I had rented the apartment. We went up the back stairs and I unlocked the door. We went inside and I turned on the light.

"The girls will be here soon," I told him. I helped him off with his coat. "A little vodka while we wait?"

"Yes," he said. He looked around the room. "Where are the others who live here?"

"No others," I said. "It is all mine while I am here. Is it not magnificent?"

"Oh, yes."

I found two glasses and poured from the vodka bottle. I handed him one of the glasses. "Everything is so much more luxurious here than in Riga. You are most fortunate."

"Moscow," he said with sudden pride, "is the most luxurious city in the world."

"To Moscow," I said, lifting my glass.

"To Moscow," he repeated, and we both drained our glasses. I immediately filled them again.

"To the socialist world," I said. Again we drank and again I filled the glasses. He might as well feel happy.

"To the women of the socialist world," I said. "May we know them for what they can be and love them for what they are."

We drank once more, but this time I drank faster than he did. I set my glass down and as he lowered his glass I was set. I swung a hard right to his jaw. The foolish smile froze on his face and he folded.

EIGHT

It was a pretty sight. When you really hit a man properly, the result is like a production by Elia Kazan. The man folds, like a beautifully constructed gimmick, gravity taking over at the point of his jaw and moving fluidly down through his body to his legs. That's the way it was with my MVD friend. He slid down an invisible pole to the floor and then slept there most peacefully.

I looked at my watch. There wasn't too much time. I had something like an hour before I was supposed to meet my black market operator to pick up the car and the papers—if any. I quickly stripped the outer clothes from the MVD man and then I tied him up with the sheet from one of the beds. A pillowcase served as a gag. I took off my own clothes and put on his uniform. It fit well enough. I also checked his papers. There was nothing about them that wouldn't pass a casual check. His full name was Alexei Sergeiev.

I left him on the floor trussed up like a chicken and went out of the apartment. I walked across the city until I came near to the Kremlin. Then I stopped in at a public phone booth. I looked up the number of the Uzbekistan Prison, dropped in fifteen kopecks, and dialed it. After a couple of rings, a man answered.

"Your director," I said roughly. "In charge of the prison tonight. What is his name?"

"Pyotr Shvernik," the man said.

"Good. Connect me with him."

As he started to make the connection, I started playing with the dial. Each time I spun it, the connection was broken. To someone on the other end it could seem to be the fault of the operator or exchange.

"Shvernik here," a man's voice said. *"U vas est telefon?"*

"Vizovite gospo—" I began and then twirled the dial so that it would cut us off. I held the dial there and gently replaced the receiver.

I waited about ten minutes, then I deposited another fifteen kopecks and dialed the prison number again. "Shvernik," I barked when the man answered.

There was a short wait. Then: "Shvernik here. Are you on the telephone?"

"Colonel Nikitin, Ministry of Internal Affairs," I said crisply. "Sergeant Sergeiev will soon be there to question the prisoner Aristova. It is important."

"Again?" he wailed. "But someone was here only an hour ago. And before that somebody from the KGB. And before that—"

"Enough," I snapped. "Do you question the order?"

"No, Colonel ..."

"Sergeant Sergeiev will be there within a few minutes," I said and hung up.

I went out and walked around the block. Then I went on to the prison. I marched in through the front door and made a sharp turn to bring up in front of the guard's booth. There was another MVD sergeant sitting behind the window.

"Sergeant Sergeiev," I announced. "I am here to interview the prisoner Aristova."

"Your papers, Sergeant."

I pulled out the sergeant's official papers and extended them. He looked at them and handed them back. He must have pressed a button, for an inner door opened and a corporal appeared.

"Sergeant Sergeiev to interview Aristova," the sergeant in the booth said.

"You wish a special room for the interview, Sergeant?"

"No," I said. "The cell will be fine. I have only a few questions. It will take only a few moments. But it must be private."

He nodded and I followed the corporal through the door. It clicked shut behind us with a grim sound that exists only in prisons. He led the way up to the second floor. I noticed that most of the cells were empty. We went about halfway down the corridor and then he indicated a cell.

"Thank you, Corporal," I said. "I'll call you when I'm ready to leave."

He nodded and turned away. I watched him until I was sure he was going back downstairs. Then I turned to her cell.

She was sitting on her cot with her face buried in her hands, paying no attention to anything. There was nobody in the cells to either side of her. I leaned up against the bars of the door.

"Zoya," I said softly.

She looked up, shock and disbelief on her face as she saw me. There were dark red bruises on her face.

"Zoya," I said quickly, "I know you could call and the

Corporal would soon be here. You would help them capture me, but it wouldn't get the paper back, and so it wouldn't really help you any. Even if I were captured, you would only be executed with me. But if you want me to, I'll help you get out of here."

She stared at me without speaking for what seemed like a long time, still not fully believing that I was there. "What do you mean?" she asked finally.

"I mean I will take you out of here," I said. "If you agree, I'll have you outside within fifteen minutes."

"Why?" she asked. "There is no place to go. They would only catch me again. And you."

"I don't think so." It was too bad I didn't feel as confident as I sounded. "I think we'll make it, honey."

"Where?"

"You could come back to America with me."

"Then you are an American?"

"Yes."

"They would only execute me as a spy," she said dully.

"No," I said. "I guarantee they won't. If you want to come to America and live there, it will be possible. You will have to give what information you have, but that is all. It will not be difficult. And I will help you." I watched the struggle taking place in her face. In the past few hours her whole world had been turned over. Until then she had been sitting on top of the world, a trusted agent who could go and come almost as she wanted. She'd even been able to afford the luxury of liking such foreign things as jazz. Then she had made her one little mistake and the only thing facing her was death or prison. I was offering her a way out of it, but one which meant reversing all the opinions she'd held all her life.

"How do I know that you speak the truth?" she asked.

"There is no way I can prove it to you," I said. "But all you have to do is think about it. I certainly didn't have to come here to offer to help you. I could have just kept on going and let you worry about yourself. But I didn't. I came here. I don't have to tell you the risk involved. You probably know it better than I do. Use the brains you have."

For a minute she wouldn't look at me. Then, finally, her gaze came up and met mine, searchingly.

"Why?" she asked.

"Why am I doing it?" She nodded. "I'm not sure. I guess part of it is that I agree that agents are a breed apart and when the chips are down should stick together. And part of it comes out of looking at you last night when you were asleep—when I got the paper."

"After you had undressed me?" she asked with a little smile.

"Yes," I admitted.

There must have been something about it that aroused the woman in her, for she was looking at me with a much softer expression. "All right," she said. "I'll go with you. But how are you going to get me out?"

"It's easy," I said. I took the lock picks from my pocket and went to work on the lock. It took about three minutes before the tumblers reacted to the piece of steel and then the door swung open. She stepped out and I closed the door. I took her by the hand and walked down the corridor. When we reached the stairs I had her wait and I went on down by myself.

The Corporal was waiting by the door. He smiled at me and started to open the door.

"Corporal," I said.

He stopped and looked at me questioningly. By that time I was up to him. "There's something I should tell you," I said and with that I struck with the edge of my palm along the side of his neck. He folded like a worn-out accordion and fell to the floor. I looked around. There was no way that any of the prisoners could see what had happened. I walked back to the stairs and motioned for Zoya to come down. She did. I told her to wait by the door and to open it when I knocked on it. She nodded. I opened the door and walked out.

"Thanks, Corporal," I called over my shoulder as I went out.

The Sergeant sat in a small cubicle or booth in the outer lobby. But I'd have to get him out of it. I thought about it as I crossed the floor toward him, then remembered one of the first things I'd been taught in OSS: always try the simple and obvious way first.

"Sergeant," I said, "could you step out here a moment? There is something I think I should tell you."

He opened the door of his cubicle and stepped out without any hesitation. "What is it?" he asked. "Something to do with the girl?"

"Yes," I said. I stepped in close to him, glancing about as though to make sure no one could hear us. As I turned back to him, I chopped my hand across his neck.

He grunted in pain, then collapsed. I caught his body as he fell, then quickly dragged him back to his cubicle. I opened the door and shoved him inside on the floor. I closed the door. No one could see him there unless he leaned inside the window and looked down. He and the Corporal would both be out long enough for us to get away from the prison.

I went back to the door connecting the prison proper and knocked on the door. It swung open and the girl looked out. She looked relieved at the sight of me.

"Come on," I said.

She stepped out and the two of us walked across the floor to the front entrance. "Where is the guard?" she asked.

"He joined the Corporal in a short siesta," I told her. "We'll talk later, but now we'd better just concentrate on getting away from here." I took her arm as we went out and down the steps. There were a few people on the streets but none of them gave a second glance to an MVD man and a girl. We walked away at a casual pace.

I would have liked to take a taxi, but it was better to walk. The driver might remember driving us and report it. So we walked across town, all the way to the room I had rented.

"The owner of this uniform is in the room," I told her as we climbed the stairs, "but I'll soon get rid of him."

I unlocked the door and we went in. I turned on a light. The man on the floor was conscious and had obviously been threshing around trying to free himself, but without any success. He glared at me over the top of the gag. I went and got a glass of water and another one of the pills I had used on the girl the night before. I squatted down beside him and took the gag off.

"Who—" he began.

"Shut up and take this," I told him.

He glanced down at the pill and clamped his jaws together stubbornly.

"I guess you'll have to help," I told the girl.

She came over obediently, although her face showed the strain she was under. The sudden switch in roles was almost too much for her. I handed her the pill and the glass of water. "Put the pill in his mouth when it opens and then give him some water," I said.

She took them and nodded. I pressed my thumbs into his jaws. He grunted with pain, but in a minute his mouth popped open. She threw the pill in and immediately tilted the glass. A lot of the water splashed over his face, but some of it went into his mouth. As soon as there was some in it, I clamped his jaws together and used my other hand to pinch his nostrils together. He threw his body around, but I had a good grip on him, so it did no good. And he couldn't take much of that. The only way he could breathe was to swallow first. His face was beginning to turn purple when he finally swallowed: I let go and immediately put the gag back in his mouth and tied it.

"I'm not interested in your opinions," I told him, "so we might as well do this until you get over the idea."

I motioned the girl to sit down and keep quiet. We sat there until the man on the floor finally relaxed. I waited another minute, then went over and lifted one eyelid. He was unconscious. I took off the gag and removed the sheet with which I'd bound him. Then I stood up and stripped off the uniform I was wearing. I got into my own clothes.

"You'll have to help me dress him," I said to the girl.

She came over without a word and the two of us managed to get him dressed again. It was quite a task. To put clothes on a completely inert body is never easy. But it was finally accomplished.

"Stay here," I said to her. "I'll be right back."

"What are you going to do with him?"

"Just leave him someplace where he can sleep it off. He'll be out for about ten hours. But he's off duty now, and if he only keeps his mouth shut, he won't get into any trouble over this."

She nodded and I lifted the man and slung him over my shoulder. I went out and down the stairs. It was late and I was fairly safe as long as I kept off the streets. I managed to find a way through backyards for two or three blocks, then I found a back doorway into which I plumped him. I arranged him so that his position wouldn't be too uncomfortable and left him that way. I went back to the room I had rented. The girl was still there. I had half expected to find her gone. I told her this.

"Where would I go?" she asked dully. "I must go with you and do what you tell me or stay here and take my punishment. It is the latter that I should do, but I don't have the courage. Still, it is true that I failed in my duty or you would not have been able to get the paper away from me. I should never have gone out with a man I didn't know when I was on an assignment."

"Nonsense," I said. "You had no way of even suspecting that someone had come after you."

"If it had happened the other way around," she asked, "would your superiors permit you to go unpunished?"

"No," I admitted, "but it wouldn't be as bad as here. They certainly wouldn't execute me for it."

"They might not have killed me either. Perhaps they would have sent me to one of the virgin lands.* As a *dobrovolno prinuditelno*." She was using a Russian expression that means "voluntarily by compulsion." I knew it applied to those who were chosen to go to such places as Siberia.

"That could also mean execution," I said. "Do you think you're equipped to survive in Siberia?"

"No," she said, "but that is only because I have been softened by the decadent living while I was in Paris. I let my socialist strength be softened by sitting in capitalistic nightclubs and listening to your savage music. And that was how you came to my apartment last night."

"You are being very foolish, Zoya," I said. "You should not be punishing yourself for enjoying a few pleasures. I thought that socialism was supposed to give all those things to everybody, not deny them to everybody."

"Does everyone have nightclubs and jazz records in your country?" she demanded.

"Not everybody," I said, "but many do who want them. Several million of them. And several million of them own television sets, washing machines, and cars. You will be able to see for yourself when you come with me. Besides, you didn't have too many luxuries for the one who is known all over Europe as The Rose."

"You know that I am The Rose?"

---

* The virgin lands were uncultivated areas that were developed into state farms in order to solve food shortages in the Soviet Union. Some of the workers sent to work in these poor conditions were released prisoners.

"Yes."

"And you say that your country still will not execute me?"

"Of course not. Even if they had caught you spying within our country, the most they would have done is send you to prison. But this is very different. You haven't been caught anywhere. You will be coming back with me voluntarily."

"*Dobrovolno prinuditelno,*" she said.

"No," I told her. "You don't have to come with me at all. You can leave anytime you want to. I rescued you from the prison because I was the cause of your being there. That's all. There's the door if you want to use it."

She looked at the door, then back to me. "What makes you think we could get out of Russia? The KGB and the MVD will turn up every clod in the Soviet Union looking for us."

"I got into Russia," I said. "I'll get out."

"How?"

"I'm getting papers in the black market for both of us, and I'm buying a car in the same place. We may not get out all the way by car, but it'll take us part of the way, and we'll get the rest of the distance covered whatever way we can make it. By foot, if necessary."

"Was there such a man as the one you pretended to be last night, or was that just an identity made up for you?"

"There was such man."

"What happened to him?"

"He is being held a prisoner at the moment by a friend of mine. As soon as I'm out of the country, he will be given a choice of returning here or going to the West."

"Your name is Milo March?" she asked.

"Yes."

"They have your fingerprints. They know who you are."

"I know," I said. "They have my fingerprints from before, when I worked in East Germany."

"Knowing that you are an American, they will do everything to stop you from leaving the country. And by tomorrow they will be releasing stories to the papers and making a complaint in the United Nations."

"I know," I said. "That adds a time factor to the problem, but that's all. I'm going out and as fast as possible. If you want to go along, fine."

She hesitated only a moment. "I'll go," she said. "I have no choice. And you're talking about a way of living that is the only way I know. So maybe we'll make it. At least, I can help."

"Good," I said. "You wait here while I go see about the car and the papers."

She nodded. I showed her the bottle of vodka and the glasses and left. I walked back to the restaurant. Nuritdin—practically my best friend by now—was standing in front of it as usual. He didn't show any particular happiness at seeing me, but he did immediately fall into step with me as we started our walk down the street.

"I hear," he said, "that there was a prison break at Uzbekistan about an hour ago."

"That's interesting," I said. "But why do you tell me?"

"That is the prison to which you bought a plan. I thought you might like to know."

"A coincidence," I said airily. "I come from a backward

republic and I only wanted to know how the prisons in Moscow are built."

"Sure," he said sarcastically. "I cannot figure you, comrade. Are you one of the foreign agents against which we are always being warned? Or are you merely one of the criminals—perhaps a chief of the *stilyagi*—whom *Pravda* is always telling us are about to be sent to prison?"

"That's easy," I said. "I'm an American capitalist on his vacation and I hate to travel any way except in luxury. And where would I find luxury except through my good friend and comrade who has his office in front of the restaurant? Which reminds me—how are things going with my luxuries?"

"You are lucky," he said sourly. "The man I approached was able to do the papers for you. I received them no more than ten minutes ago."

"I thought he might," I said dryly. "Where are they?"

"Here." He pulled them from his pocket and passed them to me. I examined them by the streetlight as we passed along. It seemed that I was going to be Alexei Mazurov, a trade representative for the cotton industry, and Zoya was going to be Tanya Kuznetsova, my secretary. It might raise a few eyebrows, but it looked all right. There were internal passports for both of us.

"There is a space provided," he said, "where each of you can place your fingerprints, using just ordinary ink. That will complete the identifications. There is ink in the apartment which you rented."

"All right," I said. I pulled money from my pocket and counted off the amount due for the papers. I handed it to him.

"There is still a small matter," he said after he had counted it, "of the money due for the car. Thirty thousand rubles."

"Minus one thousand that was given as a deposit," I pointed out.

"Minus one thousand," he agreed reluctantly.

"But I do not yet have a car," I said. I grinned at him. "When I see the car and have the keys in my hand, I will gladly give you twenty-nine thousand rubles. Until then—*nyet*."

"You lack the trust that one comrade is supposed to give another," he said. "We must go this way, then." He turned and led the way down a side street.

"One notices," he said, "that the prison break tonight at Uzbekistan was to release a girl."

"That's nice," I told him. "I am glad that our comrades still have enough feeling for women to rush to their rescue when they are put in prison."

He gave me a dirty look and kept on walking. He made another turn and I realized that we were doubling back on ourselves, walking along a street that would lead behind the restaurant. We kept going until we finally reached a rear courtyard and he turned in there. He walked up to a Pobeda parked there and slapped a fender with his hand.

"Here it is," he said.

I walked up to the small car and opened the door. I looked at the speedometer. It had the equivalent of about fifty miles on it. I went around and looked at the tires. I lifted the hood and looked at the motor. Everything looked fine.

"How do I know," I asked, "that the first time I'm stopped I won't be pulled in for driving a stolen car?"

"You don't," he said. "But this was not stolen from an individual, but from the factory. There is no record of it, so it cannot be listed as stolen. I tell you this is true, but if you do not believe me it's your privilege."

I walked around the car again, looking at it.

"The tank is full of gasoline," he said. "That was not part of the bargain, so you are getting a bonus."

"Thanks," I said dryly. I checked over the car again. If I was getting a bonus, it might mean that something else was wrong. But I couldn't find anything. Finally, I gave up and turned to him. "The keys?" I asked.

He pulled them from his pocket and handed them over. I got into the car and started the motor. It sounded fine. So then I took out my money and gave him twenty-nine thousand rubles.

"By tomorrow night," I said, "you can have the apartment back. I will be gone by then."

"All right," he said stolidly. "You will not be around again?"

"Probably not," I said. "But don't let it give you any ideas. If the KGB catches me because of black market dealings, I'll be sure to tell them where I bought everything."

"You do me wrong, comrade," he said with a wounded expression. "I would not do such a thing."

"Just so we understand each other," I said. "Well, good-bye. It's been nice doing business with you."

"I cannot say the same," he said honestly. "It is true that I have made a nice profit from you in a short period of time, but you make me nervous, comrade. I confess that I will be glad that you are not to be around in the future. But I wish you good luck, comrade."

"Thanks."

"It is also rumored," he said, with a sly smile, "that the girl who escaped from the prison was aided by an American spy."

"Ah, those mad Americans," I said. "They will do anything to get into the newspapers. *Dasvidanya.*"

"Good-bye," he repeated.

I slammed the door shut and drove away. A few minutes later I parked the car in the rear of the building where I had the apartment. I locked it and went upstairs. The dark-haired girl was sitting on the bed, sipping a glass of vodka. I poured a glass for myself and sat down next to her.

"Well, we have new identification papers," I told her. I took them out and tossed them over to her. "We still have to put our fingerprints on them, but otherwise how do they look?"

She examined them carefully. "Pretty good," she said finally. "Where did you get them?"

"In the black market."

"There is no black market in Russia," she said promptly.

"No?" I asked with a grin. "Then I must have paid twenty thousand rubles to the government for those papers and another thirty thousand rubles for the car that's waiting for us downstairs."

"Fifty thousand rubles?" she asked. "You've really spent that much money to try to get us out?"

"I also bought a plan of the prison," I said lightly, "and it will cost me a lot more before we're out. So what? You know how it is with those rich, capitalistic Americans."

She looked at me quizzically.

"But enough of that," I said. "What about the papers? Think they'll pass?"

"Probably," she said. "But the fingerprints may not. They have mine and they claim to have yours."

"I had a sort of idea about that," I said. "You have fairly large hands for a woman and mine are only average. So maybe we'll put your prints on my papers and mine on yours. Unless we get a guy who's imaginative, they'll certainly pass anything short of a thorough investigation."

She thought about it a minute. "That's smart," she finally admitted. "If we're stopped, it'll probably be by the MVD, and they may not be smart enough to think of that."

I didn't bother to tell her that the KGB probably wouldn't either. She might as well lose her illusions bit by bit.

"But how do you plan to get out?" she asked.

"Frankly, I don't know," I said. I grinned at her. "We're going to leave Moscow and head south and keep going until we're inside the territory of some Western country—probably Turkey."

"Why south?"

"It's as good as any other direction," I said. "Besides, it's the one direction they'll least suspect me of taking."

"Why?"

"The man whose identity I took came from Azerbaijan. Since they know that I'm aware that they know who I am, they will be certain to think that I will be careful not to head in that direction. So I will."

She nodded. "Where?"

"I'm not too sure," I said. "I've been thinking roughly of heading down through Tula, Yelets, Voronezh, Rostov, Kushchevskaya, and Kropotkin. At Kropotkin we can either cross

Mount Elbrus to Batumi, Georgia, and then cross over the border to Turkey, or we can cut over to Novorossiysk and try to cross the Black Sea to Turkey."

"I think the Black Sea is better," she said.

"Maybe," I said. "I think we'll have to wait until we get there and see which is the safer. A lot of things can happen between here and Kropotkin."

"Whatever you think best," she said.

"Look, honey," I said, "I wasn't meaning to ignore your ideas. There will be a lot of things on which your ideas are going to be best—maybe this is one of them. All I'm really saying is that we need to wait and decide according to other things that happen. Our situation may change from hour to hour. What do you think about us leaving now? Or would it be better to leave in the day?"

She thought about it for a minute. "With these papers we could leave now," she said. "It would not be unusual for such a trade representative to leave at night and take his secretary along. And in a way it might be better. They might think that you couldn't get false papers so quickly. I am surprised myself."

"I paid double for them," I said. "That's all. Plain old-fashioned capitalism will sometimes produce miracles."

"What kind of car do you have?" she asked.

"A Pobeda."

"That's good," she said, nodding. "That's about what you should have for what you are pretending to be. I can see that you are planning well." She hesitated a minute. "Do you work for the American Central Intelligence Agency?"

"Yes," I said. "At least I do now. I do not work for it all the time."

"I do not understand."

"I used to work for OSS," I explained. "Then I left the army and went back to my regular job. Now they call me back once in a while when they have a special job for me to do. But that's all. The last time I worked for the CIA was two or three years ago when I went to East Berlin."

"What is your regular job?" she asked.

"An insurance investigator. It's probably a job you wouldn't understand, but I'll explain it to you later. We'll have plenty of time."

"How did you know where to find me?" she asked curiously.

"I'm afraid I tricked your friend in Paris."

"Maryutka?"

I nodded. "I made her think that I was a KGB man who had been in America for five years and no longer knew any girls in Moscow. Since she already had discovered that the three of us liked jazz, she thought it might be an excellent idea if we got together."

"You must have been very clever to fool her," she said. "Maryutka is smart. But even if she was fooled, it's strange that she didn't get some word to me."

"I expect," I said, "she discovered that she'd been tricked and didn't want to expose herself. Maybe she hoped that I'd never get through to you and so she just kept her mouth shut."

"Perhaps," she said.

"We'd better get started," I told her. "It's going to be a long trip. I suggest that you look around and see if there are some clothes here that you can wear. A description of what you're wearing will probably be circulated."

She nodded and started looking. After a while she came up with three dresses that would fit her. None of them was too bad.

"It will be all right to take them?" she asked.

"Sure," I said. "I've paid enough for this room to cover them, but we'll leave them a few extra rubles anyway." She quickly stripped off her own clothes and put on one of the dresses. She also found a good heavy sweater to wear with it. She made a bundle of the other dresses and indicated she was ready. I counted a thousand rubles and left them lying on the table. Then we went out and down the stairs. We got into the car and drove off.

I drove across the city until I hit Gorky Street, then stayed on it until it became Leningrad Chaussee, the special highway that connects Moscow and Leningrad.

"Too bad we can't stay on this," I said, "but we'll head south as soon as we get outside the city."

"Do you know the way?" she asked.

"No," I said cheerfully, "but I figure that in any good socialist state there ought to be markers. If not, we'll ask questions—unless I'm so lucky that you know the way."

"I know it as far as Yelets," she said. "After that, I do not know any of the roads."

"Then we'll just point the nose of the car south and follow it," I said.

She looked at me curiously. "Are all Americans like you?" she asked.

"I hope not," I said. "If they were, think of the trouble I'd have trying to find someone to go out with on a date." For the first time since I'd met her, she laughed.

The main part of the city had already dropped behind us and we were nearing the outskirts. There were practically no other cars on the road. Once a big Zis roared past us, rocking from one side of the road to the other, but that was the only car we saw in several miles.

We rounded a gradual curve in the street, and there ahead of us were the city limits. The streetlights were dim here, but they were bright enough for me to see that there was more than just city limits ahead. A Zis limousine was drawn squarely across the road and several uniformed men stood beside the car. It was a roadblock.

NINE

As soon as I saw it, I cut the speed. There was no point in waiting for any sort of signal; a roadblock speaks an international language. And I was sure that any Russian would get ready to stop at the sight of one without needing to be told by a policeman. Zoya stirred on the seat beside me.

"I'm frightened," she said.

"It'll be all right," I said. "I'm sure that they won't go much beyond looking at our papers, but if they do, just use your head. I'm sure you can handle anything that comes up in direct questioning of you. I'll try to handle everything else."

"You'll have to," she said. There was a hint of a smile in her voice. "No secretary in Russia would make explanations on such a trip as this will seem to be, except when questions are asked her."

"All right," I said. "Here we go."

I braked gradually, bringing the car to a slow stop near the policemen. I stopped a little short of the exact spot where they stood, so there was actually room for me to send the car hurtling around the Zis that blocked the main part of the road. As I stopped, I shifted the car into gear and held it there. I managed to do that before the MVD sergeant reached the window on my side. I noticed that another man was at the other window and the rest of them stayed in front of us.

"Your papers, please," the sergeant said gruffly.

I handed over mine and took Zoya's from her and gave them to him. "What's the trouble, Sergeant?" I asked.

"There is no trouble," he said sharply. He took the papers and stepped ahead of the car to examine them. The other MVD man stayed beside the car. The sergeant went over the papers carefully, stopping several times to look at some papers of his own. Finally he came back to the car and flashed a light on us. He studied us for two or three minutes in the pitiless glare of the big flashlight. It was a tough few minutes and I was ready to send the car lunging ahead at the slightest warning that he'd spotted us. I'd figured out that we could get away, although whether we could then stay ahead of the Zis was another matter.

"Where are you going?" he asked finally.

"Eventually to Batumi in Georgia," I said, "but there are many stops to make before then."

"Why are you traveling at night?" he asked.

"So as to be in Tula early in the morning," I said. I squirmed in my seat and acted embarrassed, glancing at the girl beside me. "Then, too, Sergeant," I said nervously, making my voice even lower, "my secretary has just started working for me and I thought I would like the chance to get acquainted with her before we started to work in the morning. You know how it is."

He flashed the light on Zoya again, then it seemed to me that he relaxed somewhat. "Such socialist zeal in going to work at night," he said, "should be rewarded in some way. But perhaps it carries, its own reward, eh, comrade?"

"I think so," I murmured.

"We mustn't stand in the way of such socialistic endeavor," he said. He handed the papers back to me. "You may go, comrade. Do not work too hard in the cotton fields." He laughed loudly, pleased by his own wit.

I handed Zoya's papers back to her and put my own away in my pocket. All I wanted to do was get out of there, but it wouldn't be good for him to notice that I was in a hurry. Then I made a show of putting the car in gear, even though it already was. By that time the other MVD men had moved out of the way. I stepped on the accelerator and the car moved slowly forward as I skirted around the Zis.

Another minute and we were on the other side of it and picking up speed.

"You did that very well," Zoya said. "It was just the right note to make him believe we were just what we pretend to be."

"Thanks," I said. "But I don't think I can take all the credit. When I handed him my papers there was five hundred rubles folded up inside. They weren't there when he returned the papers."

"Where did you learn so much about how to handle the MVD?" she asked sarcastically.

"People—and especially cops—are pretty much the same all over the world.

Most people don't mind picking up a few extra dollars if they don't have to do too much for it."

"But it was dangerous," she said. "It might have been just the thing to make him suspicious of us."

"No," I said. "He was looking for an American spy. If a spy was expecting to buy his way through a blockade, he'd offer several thousand rubles, not a paltry five hundred. That's about how much a man on a mild escapade would offer not to be embarrassed."

"I suppose so," she admitted. "We turn to the left about a half mile from here."

I slowed down, watching for the sign, and soon saw the arrow pointing south and the name Tula. I swung off on a small, narrow, but well-paved road. We were well out in the country now and there were no lights except those of our car. Nowhere was there even a sign of another car.

"What about this section?" I asked her. "Are there apt to be MVD patrols?"

"Not normally," she said. "Unless they're on special orders, there won't be any in the rural sections. There may be a few around in Tula, but they'll be only those who are on regular night duty."

"Then we should be all right," I said. I stepped on the gas, sending the little car hurtling along the road as fast as it would go. "They certainly missed you within a half hour after we left the prison. The two guards would not have remained unconscious longer than that. They'd probably feel pretty certain that we hadn't gotten out of the city by that time. What they probably did was throw guards at every possible exit from the city and that was why we ran into a roadblock."

"I suppose so," she admitted.

"It'll be sometime tomorrow before they conclude that we managed to get out of the city," I said. "So we'll be relatively safe until then. After that, it may be a different story. But in the meantime I think you can relax."

"Thanks," she said softly.

"Don't thank me until we're out," I grunted. After that I turned my full attention to driving. Zoya curled up on the seat and was silent.

We made the run to Tula without incident and without ever seeing a car or a single person. When we reached Tula, I slowed down and drove sedately through the streets. A glance at the instruments showed me that we didn't need any gasoline. I wouldn't have minded stopping for a drink, but it was late and so far as I could see, there wasn't a single place open. Once I saw a uniformed MVD man; he glanced curiously at the car, but that was all. As soon as we hit the open road again, I pushed the accelerator to the floor.

We'd been on the road just six and a half hours, and it was daylight when we reached Yelets. I drove slowly down the main street, looking at the signs.

"What are we going to do now?" Zoya asked.

"Later on today it's liable to start getting rugged," I said, "so I think we'd better stop here and get five or six hours' sleep. I'm looking for a hotel now."

A couple of blocks farther on, I found one. It looked as if it might be the best one I could find in a city of this size. I found a place to park the car on a side street near the hotel and we walked to it. I showed our identification cards to the clerk and told him I'd like quarters for my secretary and myself. I signed us in and then we were taken upstairs.

To my surprise we were both ushered into a single big

room, with a large double bed, and left there. I looked at Zoya.

"They must have misunderstood me," I said. "I said I wanted quarters for both of us and I meant separate rooms."

She laughed. "In most places this is the arrangement they expect when a businessman shows up with his secretary. Do they not do such things in America?"

"Yes, but he's apt to run into a little trouble if he says she's his secretary. If he has something like this in mind, he usually registers as husband and wife."

"Hypocrites," she said scornfully.

"Anyway," I said, "I'm sorry, Zoya. I'll go down and talk to them about it."

"You'd better not," she said. "That would make them suspicious. It just might seem so unusual to them that they'd go to the MVD."

"Well … ," I said uncertainly. "You're sure you don't mind? There seems to be only one bed."

"I don't mind," she said. She seemed to be amused at me.

I looked the room over. It wasn't bad. Everything in it was very old, but it was clean. I checked the bathroom. The fixtures were also old, but they were in working condition. There was even a shower attachment.

"There appears to be a shower that works," I told Zoya. "You want to go first?"

"You go ahead," she said. She was sitting on the edge of the bed, combing her dark hair.

I went into the bathroom, undressed, and took a shower. The water was even fairly hot, and I came out of it feeling much better.

"Your turn," I said, going back into the room. She nodded and went into the bathroom without speaking. I got into bed, turning on my side, with my back toward the middle of the bed. I was tired enough so that the bed felt good; it wasn't going to be difficult for me to get to sleep.

I was just drifting off when I felt her get into the bed.

"Milo," she said after a minute.

"Huh?" I grunted.

"Milo," she repeated softly. "I'm lonely. ..."

So I turned over and took her in my arms. Her hair brushed across my face and there was a nice scent to it. Her body was soft and warm. I wasn't as sleepy as I'd thought I was.

I awakened automatically a little more than five hours later. I looked down at Zoya. She was still asleep, one arm curled around her head, a half smile on her face. I reached over and stroked her hair until she stirred and finally opened her eyes. There was fear in them when they first opened, but it soon fled.

"For a minute I thought I had imagined all of it," she said, "and I was back in the prison."

"No, honey," I said. "You didn't imagine any of it. But now we have to get started. We've still got two or three days ahead of us, and there's always a chance that we'll both be back in that prison of yours. So get a move on."

She jumped out of bed and ran to the bathroom. It was far enough for me to get a good look at her. She had a beautiful body and it moved with the grace of a dancer. She must have known that I was looking at her, for she laughed softly without glancing around. Then the door slammed and the shower was turned on.

Within a few minutes we both were dressed and went downstairs. It was just lunchtime, so we went into the dining room and ate. Afterward we went out and walked to the car. It hadn't been bothered. I found a place to buy some gasoline. Then we stopped at a government store and bought some clothes for her and a couple of shirts and some socks for me. On the way back to the car I bought a local newspaper, but there was nothing in it about us. We got back into the car and once more headed south.

"Milo," she asked once we were out of the city, "are you sure I won't go to prison in your country also?"

"Positive," I said. "At least, if you do as I tell you. You will have to give all the information you can about the KGB and about any other agents you know."

"But that will make me a traitor to my own country," she said in a small voice.

"You are already considered a traitor in your own country," I said gently. "If I hadn't taken you out of that prison, you probably would have died for it. Or, at the best, gotten something like thirty years in prison."

"But it wasn't my fault. It wasn't something I did."

"You and I know that," I told her, "but was the KGB going to pay any attention to it? Or would the judges? Did the KGB give you credit for that when they arrested you?"

"No," she said. She shuddered on the seat beside me. "You must give me time, Milo. I know you are right, but it seems so unreal. It was only two days ago that I was a trusted agent, given all sorts of special privileges and awards—and now ..." Her voice trailed off as she stared out the window.

"And what will happen to me," she asked finally, "after I have told your government all the things they want to know?"

"First, you'll be granted political asylum. Later, if you want to, you can become a citizen. Other Russians have."

"And how will I feed myself? What work will I do? I have never been trained for anything but working in the KGB. So what can I do? Become the mistress of some fat American capitalist?"

"You might become the mistress of a skinny one," I said. "But if you want to work, there are probably dozens of things you can do. I might even give you a job myself."

"Then you are also an American capitalist?"

"Not as you've been taught the word," I said. "But I do have my own insurance investigating agency, as I told you, and maybe I can give you a job when you're ready to take one. Your KGB training would come in handy there."

"What do you do?" she asked.

For the next hour I explained to her what an insurance investigator did. By then we had reached Voronezh and apparently everything was still all right. Nobody gave us a second glance as we drove down the street. Maybe, I told myself, we could make it before the police got the manhunt under way. We weren't too far from the Black Sea, about seven hundred miles at a rough estimate, and only a little farther from the Georgia-Turkey border. But even as I told myself, I knew I was probably only kidding myself. The Russian secret police were smart, and they'd probably have the whole country blanketed long before that.

We stopped in Voronezh long enough to pick up a bottle of

vodka and we both had a few drinks as we drove away.

While we weren't able to make as good time as we had the night before, there wasn't too much traffic on the road and very few villages, so in another four hours we were approaching Markovka.

I had decided we would stop and have dinner in Markovka and see if there was any news. If things looked clear, we could then go on and maybe even make Rostov before we knocked off. That would be another two hundred miles and would make a good day's traveling over those Russian roads.

We were barely inside Markovka when I sighted a small restaurant that looked ideal. From the outside, at least, it looked clean and pleasant. I parked the car and we went in. I knew I'd picked well the minute we entered. The place was spotlessly clean and we could smell the cooking food. There was a good smell to it.

There were no other customers yet, possibly because it was still a little early. We sat down at one of the tables and in a moment a little, rosy-cheeked woman came bustling out of the kitchen to greet us. In answer to my questions she told us that she and her daughter ran the restaurant by themselves and that she did all the cooking herself. She apologized for the fact that she didn't serve any liquor, but she said that we could drink our own if we liked and she would give us glasses. I got up and went out to the car to get our bottle of vodka.

When I returned she had already brought glasses and was polishing them briskly with her apron while she talked to Zoya.

"Your wife tells me, *grajdanin*," she said, "that you are from Moscow."

I glanced at Zoya. Then I decided she must have decided that this was a place where the employer-secretary story wouldn't go so well. Or she was becoming Americanized faster than I had expected her to.

"That is true," I said. I didn't say any more, not knowing what else Zoya may have told her.

"It is on pleasure that you visit our Markovka?" she asked.

"No," I said. I offered her some of the vodka but she refused. I poured some for Zoya and myself. "We are on business of the government. We must go on to the south immediately after we have had dinner."

She clucked her tongue sympathetically. "It is too bad. You and your wife would like Markovka. But if you are just from Moscow, you must know all about the excitement."

I sent a warning glance at Zoya. "I'm afraid not," I said. "We left Moscow late last night and we have not heard any news since then. Is it another threat of war? Or has Tito come to his senses?"

"Oh, nothing like that," she said. "It seems that there is an American spy in Russia. Imagine that."

"Really," I said as if I didn't believe it.

"Not only in Russia, but he may be right here in Markovka," she said triumphantly. "It was on the radio this afternoon, and since then the whole town has talked of nothing else."

"But why here?" I asked. "Are there secrets to be obtained in Markovka?"

"Oh, no," she said. "It is said that the American was in

Moscow and was being helped by a girl who had worked for our own police—can you imagine such a thing? The girl was arrested and then the American knocked out two brave policemen—just like an American gangster—and took the girl away. It was reported that they are headed this way in a car hoping to get over the border. Just think of it. Never has Markovka known such excitement."

I could see a look of fear beginning to appear on Zoya's face and I nudged her with my knee under the table. I lifted my glass of vodka.

"To the brave defenders of the Motherland," I said solemnly. Zoya and I drank. "Do they at least know what these two spies look like?" I asked the woman.

"They described them on the radio," she said. "Of course, it is difficult to go by such descriptions. The American is a young man something like yourself and the girl is dark-haired and pretty like your wife. It is hard to tell more."

I had to nudge Zoya again. I realized, of course, that the woman wouldn't even think of us as being the two she was talking about, mostly because I spoke good Russian and she couldn't imagine an American doing that. There were also thousands of Americans in America who wouldn't be able to imagine a Russian speaking with an American accent.

"They will be caught," I said confidently. "You may be sure of that. Our police will think of something to do."

"It is said that they already have," she said. "It is that which the entire town is talking about. Not more than two hours ago, they brought in more policemen and they have blocked the road as one leaves Markovka for the south. It is said that they are so sure the two are near here that the MVD have set up their headquarters in Kamenskaya, only one hundred kilometers south of here. It is an important day for Markovka. You and your wife are lucky to visit us on such a day."

"Very lucky," I agreed solemnly. "How do they know that the two spies are coming here?"

"I do not know," she said. "They did not say on the radio."

"They will catch them," I said. "If not here, then somewhere else. But you, Little Mother, should be more careful in talking about it. One never knows to whom one talks."

"Oh, I'm most careful," she said. "But one knows one's own people when talking to them. Now I will get your dinner." She bustled back to the kitchen.

"Milo, what will we do?" Zoya asked in a small voice.

"First," I said, "we'll have some more vodka and then we will eat our dinner. After dinner, we'll worry. If a man has to die, he does it much better on a full stomach." I gave her a grin and poured some more vodka.

"But won't she start getting suspicious about us? After all, we are strangers."

"Probably not. At least, not until it's too late. You were smart to tell her we're husband and wife. She sees a nice Russian girl who couldn't possibly be the kind that was described on the radio. And I speak pretty good Russian and don't seem to have horns, so she can't imagine that I'm an American spy. Most people in most countries think that villains have a special look."

"Maybe," she said. She made an attempt to smile. "But we still have to think of something to do."

"After dinner," I said firmly. "Man not only dies better but thinks better on a full stomach. So the first thing we do is have a good dinner."

And have a good dinner we did. First we had a thick meat soup, then stuffed cabbage plus kasha, and we polished it off with homemade ice cream and coffee. It was a pretty expensive meal by American standards, but it was cheap according to Moscow prices. I left a generous tip for the woman and her daughter, assured her that we'd stop on our way back, then picked up the rest of our vodka and left. Back in the car, I sat for a moment before starting the motor.

"We really have only two choices," I said finally. "We can turn around and go back, trying to get out another way. But at the best that can only win us a few hours. I don't know how they got us spotted, but they have. If they have us located, they may also have a description of our car, so pretty soon we'll have to change our method of travel. And I don't think we'll gain anything by just turning around and running."

"What is our other choice?" she asked calmly.

"To try to go ahead. Of course, we'll have to get a look at the roadblock, but just getting the look will almost force us to go ahead unless it's completely impossible—like a solid concrete wall. I doubt very much if we can bluff our way through. They probably don't know the names we're using, but the descriptions may very well make up for that. Unfortunately, I don't have a gun and I don't suppose we can pick one up in Markovka. But I still think that we may do better trying to run ahead than to run away."

"Whatever you say, Milo," she said. "I think you are probably right. I'm sorry that I was frightened back in the restaurant. I promise you that it will not happen again."

"It's all right, honey," I said. "I'm scared myself." I leaned over and kissed her. "Shall we go?"

"Yes," she said firmly. "It is the best plan always to go ahead. You do whatever you think best and I will try my best to help."

"Good girl," I said. I started the car and we drove slowly down the main street. I watched until I caught sight of a government store. I parked again and went into the store, leaving Zoya in the car. It took me only a few minutes to make my purchases and then I was back. I slipped behind the wheel and we were off. I could feel the muscles in my stomach curling up in tension. In a way it was a good feeling. Something was about to happen and that was usually better than just waiting for something to happen.

Finally we reached the edge of Markovka, and there ahead the road stretched to the south. Or almost stretched ahead. A high wooden fence had been built across it and ten or twelve armed uniformed men stood in front of it. To one side stood a black Zim sedan.

TEN

There wasn't much time to make a decision. The barricade was maybe two hundred yards ahead. If I turned around and tried to go back, the men would probably open fire. So in a way, the decision was already made. I kept driving straight on, slowly slackening speed as a normally unguilty driver might do.

"Hold tight, baby," I said. "We're about to try to prove that the hand is mightier than the sword—or something like that."

The MVD men were all very much at attention, their guns held in readiness as I approached. One of them, in the center, was waving his gun for me to stop even though he could see that I was already obeying.

I was glad of one thing, but even there I was kidding myself. Their car was a Zim and not a Zis, which meant that it wasn't as fast. But it probably was still twenty miles an hour faster than the Pobeda I was driving, so it was only a relative joy.

When I was about twenty yards from the barricade, and the speedometer had dropped to about ten miles an hour (and why I ever bothered to translate kilometers into miles at that point I'll never know), I breathed a small prayer to anyone who cared to listen, pushed in the clutch, and shifted to second gear. The prayer was that it wouldn't make any noise.

It didn't. I promised myself I'd light a candle at the first Coca-Cola station I came to.

As it became obvious that I was stopping, the policemen relaxed slightly and began to move to converge on the car when it came to a full stop. It was now or never.

"Get down on the seat," I ordered Zoya.

Out of the corner of my eye, I saw her obey. Then I let the clutch out, took my foot off the brake, and jammed the accelerator all the way to the floor. The rest was all confusion.

The motor roared and the Pobeda leaped forward like a startled rabbit. There was a brief second when the policemen looked unbelievingly at the car and then tried simultaneously to get out of the way and bring their guns up to shoot me. It was a difficult combination. They didn't quite make it.

I felt rather than saw the two front fenders catch policemen on either side and toss them away. Then the fence loomed up through the windshield and I hunched down in the seat as far as I could. The car hit the fence, hesitated a moment, then bucked its way through to the sound of breaking wood and crumpling steel. The wheels bounced over pieces of wood and the steering wheel writhed in my grip, but I managed to keep the car on the road. We were still picking up speed.

There were small popping sounds from behind us and suddenly one section of the windshield dissolved in front of me. A splinter of glass, from somewhere, raked painfully across the back of my neck.

The motor was straining. I quickly shifted to high and pushed the accelerator again. The car responded nobly.

There were still popping sounds from behind us, but they

were fainter and no more glass vanished in front of my eyes. Then the sounds stopped and there was a merciful curve in the road.

"Are you all right, Zoya?" I asked.

"Yes," she said faintly. "Are you?"

"I think so," I said. "I may have lost a few years of my life and I think I got a small scratch on the back of my neck, but otherwise I'm fine, I think."

I could feel her suddenly sit up beside me and then her soft fingers were at my neck. "It's bleeding," she said. She started dabbing at it with something.

"So it's bleeding," I said. "Right now I need a cigarette worse than I do first aid. Reach in my shirt pocket, get one, and light it for me. Besides, the blood is probably half alcohol anyway and we may need it before we're through with this."

She stopped fooling with my neck and reached for the cigarettes. She lit one and stuck it between my lips. The first sharp bite of the smoke felt good.

"It's not bleeding badly," she said, but she was dabbing at it again. "That was very good, Milo, but you know they'll be after us by now and that Zim is much faster than this."

"I know," I grunted. I rounded another curve in the road and then took my foot off the gas. I began braking as fast as it was safe to do.

"What are you going to do?" she asked.

"Stop them," I said. "I hope." I brought the Pobeda to a full stop, set the brake, and jumped out, leaving the motor running. I took the package I had bought in Markovka with me and went back behind the car. I dumped the contents of all the boxes all over the road. I threw the boxes away and went back to the car. Within a few minutes we had resumed full speed.

"What did you do?" she asked.

"Wait," I said. When I'd stopped, I'd heard the distant whine of a speeding car, and now I was waiting to hear something else.

Shortly there was an explosive sound, then a distant screeching as though steel and rubber were being tested to the utmost, followed by a resounding crash.

"Good," I said. "Business is picking up."

"What happened?" she asked.

"We had no weapons, so I had to fall back on an old-fashioned remedy," I said. "When I stopped in the store in Markovka I bought all the carpet tacks they had. Thirty-five boxes of them. I spread them all across the road when I stopped. Our MVD friends just got one or more flat tires, which wrecked them. And now I need a drink of vodka."

She passed me the bottle and I took a good stiff drink without slackening speed.

It helped to stop some of the shaking that was going on inside of me as a reaction to the tension which we had just been through.

"Thanks, honey," I said, handing the bottle back. "Now, all of this doesn't buy a damn thing except some time. But we can use that. We've stopped them from chasing us in that Zim which could have caught us. Sure, they'll probably get another car in Markovka and come on, but that'll take them long enough so they won't catch up. And sure they'll call ahead to Kamenskaya, so we're caught in between them. But we still have more time than we had ten minutes ago."

"So what do we do?"

"I don't really know," I confessed. "But that's the way I work. If I know one step at a time, that's enough. All I know now is that we'll get as close to Kamenskaya as we can. Then we get rid of this car and go on in on foot. After that we'll have to play it whatever way seems the best. The trouble with making too many plans is that you often are stuck with them just because you made them."

"Whatever you say," she said. "I'm beginning to understand how you managed to reach Moscow and to get the paper from me. I'm also beginning to see why you were assigned to come after me. You are a good agent, Milo. There have been many agents assigned to get me in Europe and not one came close. I'm not such a big fool as you made me seem to be."

"I know you're not, honey," I said gently. "Don't worry about it. I was lucky, too."

"I don't think it was so much luck. I am glad that there may be a chance for me to work with you in America. There will be a chance, won't there? You weren't just telling me that to make me feel good?"

"There'll be a chance," I assured her.

She chattered on for several minutes while I concentrated on the driving. I kept the Pobeda at top speed, taking the curves with squealing rubber. Finally she fell silent, and I didn't interrupt her thoughts except to ask her twice for a cigarette.

We made the trip in a little under an hour. As soon as I saw we were drawing near Kamenskaya, I slowed up and began to watch the road. When we were about a half mile from the edge of Kamenskaya, I saw a spot that looked all right. There was a forest on one side of the highway, and a narrow dirt road wound in through the middle of it. I braked the car to a crawl and turned in on it. I drove along it for three or four hundred yards, then turned off and drove into the forest. I dodged between trees until I could finally go no farther. I switched off the motor and threw the keys away.

"Come on," I said. "This is not the best place in the world to hide the car, but it'll have to do. They probably won't find it until sometime tomorrow. By then we shouldn't care."

She got out of the car and we went back to the highway and started walking toward the city.

"If we hear a car coming before we reach the city," I said, "we get off the road and hide as quickly as possible. But once we reach the city, we'll have a chance."

"To do what?" she asked.

"Maybe to spend the night or maybe to steal another car and get some new papers if we need them. The first thing to do is try to learn what they do know about us. By this time there ought to be something in the newspapers, don't you think?"

She nodded. "But it may not tell us all they know. The story will contain only what the MVD wants to have appear."

"I realize that, but if they do know the names we're using, they'll probably want them included. It will make it easier for others to spot us."

We reached the town without anyone coming along. It was getting dark. I began to breathe a little easier. As soon as we hit the city limits, we switched over to another street. We walked casually along, holding hands. We finally reached a place where we could buy a newspaper. I bought the local paper. We went on until we came to a small, dingy café. We went in and ordered two bottles of beer and I opened the paper.

There was a story on us. We read it together. They had plenty of information, including a description of the car we had been driving and the names we were using. The story told how we had managed to get out of Moscow because of the forged papers but that they knew about us thanks to the splendid work of Sergeant Kedrov, who, when it was known that the spies had slipped out of Moscow, remembered the man and woman who had driven past his post.

"So I threw away five hundred rubles," I said bitterly. "I have an old-fashioned feeling that when a cop is bought, he should stay bought."

She laughed.

The rest of the story merely told what area we were in and promised that the two spies would soon be caught. It ended with the information that a formal protest was being made in the United Nations and to the American government over a known American agent, the infamous Milo March, being sent into Soviet territory. That last little bit was probably soon going to have General Roberts sweating over his answers.

We finished our beer and left the café.

"Well," I said, "that simplifies what we have to do. For one thing, we have to get new papers or we won't even be able to register in a hotel."

"How will we get them?" she asked.

"Even if this town has a black market, it probably doesn't boast of such fancy things as forged papers. So I expect we'll have to find a couple of innocent citizens and knock them over their heads to get their papers. I don't like to do it, but—wait a minute."

We had reached the main part of town and were just passing a big hotel. Parked directly in front of it was a big black Zis.

"Correct me if I'm wrong," I said. "The Zis is a car driven only by government officials, isn't it? Ordinary Russians, even if they have money, can't even buy one."

"That is true," she said. She bent to look closer at the plates on the car. "This one belongs to the Ministry of Internal Affairs at Stalingrad."

"That's the MVD?"

"Yes. They've probably sent a number of MVD men into this area from Stalingrad to make sure of catching us. Since there wouldn't be any official of importance here, they probably sent someone from Stalingrad to oversee the capture."

"And one can guess," I said, "that he's inside having a good dinner or maybe even making this his headquarters so he can be comfortable while he waits for reports. Is there anyplace we can leave these and pick them up later?" I indicated our extra clothes, which were tied up in a bundle.

She looked around and nodded. She took the bundle from me and went across the street. I watched her go into a small store and when she came out she no longer carried it.

"I asked the lady in the store to keep it for us," she said. "I told her that my husband and I had to see about a job and didn't want to carry it around with us. It's done quite often."

"Good girl," I said.

"Why did you want to get rid of the clothes?" she asked.

"We're going in to have a second dinner," I said. "We can't register and it might look strange if we carried them into the dining room."

"But you just said that the MVD official might be in there having dinner."

"That's why we're going in," I said. "We might learn more about what they plan. Besides, what safer place could we find, while we make our own plans, than right next to the man who is in charge of looking for us? Nobody will look for us there."

I could see the idea frightened her, but she had plenty of nerve. She merely nodded and went along with me into the hotel. We marched through the lobby and on to the dining room. We entered slowly so that I would have a chance to look around.

The dining room was about half full, but it wasn't difficult to spot the man we were looking for. He was the one getting all the service. At least four waiters were hovering around him. He was a heavyset man of about fifty or fifty-five, and there was an air of authority in the expression on his face.

We walked across the dining room and took a table next to his. One of the waiters frowned at us as if to scare us away, but we ignored him and sat down. It then took a little finger-snapping to get a waiter, but finally one consented to come over and get our order. I told him to bring us two orders of Stolichny vodka and two orders of fresh caviar. I thought I'd better make the drinks double since the waiters were so busy; then Zoya looked as if she needed it. She was pale, although that was the only indication that she was frightened.

The waiter was soon back with our order. By this time, we had attracted a certain amount of attention even from our neighbor. The combination of taking the table we had— whereas the average Russian is more apt to stay away from anyone who looks like an official—the finger-snapping for the waiter, and our order, which I'd given in a loud voice, had taken care of that. But I pretended not to be aware that anyone was looking at us. I lifted my vodka, clicking the glass with Zoya's, and drank deeply. I was glad to see that some color began to creep into Zoya's cheeks after she had her drink.

Without ever really looking directly at our neighbor, I soon discovered that he was eating a large meal and washing it down with copious amounts of vodka. I began to get a glimmer of an idea, although I'd still have to find some way to bring it off.

I called the waiter in a loud voice and ordered two more vodkas. I asked the waiter if he was the man who had waited on us the night before. He didn't think so. I insisted. Up to that point he had been certain that he had never seen me before, but he began to have doubts in face of my confidence. By the time he went to get the drinks he was even beginning to think he might have served us the night before.

We were halfway through our second drinks when an MVD captain strode into the dining room. He looked around until he spotted our neighbor and walked briskly over. The waiters scattered like quail. The captain saluted and began to speak.

He was keeping his voice low, but we were near enough so that I could hear him.

"… seem to have vanished between Markovka and here," he was saying. "There's no place they could go, but they may be hiding out somewhere along the road. The detachment at Markovka is on its way. I've just sent some of my men out to start searching from this end."

"Send out more," our neighbor snapped. "But find them quickly. I don't want to have to spend the rest of my life in this miserable town."

"Yes, sir," the Captain said.

"One more thing, Captain," the man said. "I think you might be even more uncomfortable in Siberia than I am here in this town. I trust you understand."

"Yes, sir," the Captain repeated. His face was pale and tight. He saluted again, but the man had already gone back to his eating and the Captain left.

I waited a few minutes, drinking my vodka, then I leaned over toward the next table. "Pardon me, sir," I said.

He lifted his head and stared at me with cold, angry eyes. "Yes?" he asked roughly.

"My wife and I could not help overhearing your conversation with the Captain," I said. "I just wanted to say that we appreciate your feelings about this town and that we hope that you will soon capture those two vicious spies. With you in charge, we are sure you will. I was wondering if we might buy a drink for a true hero of the Soviet Union?"

His gaze bored into mine with no change of expression. "Are you a native of this area?"

"No," I said. "We are from Moscow. I am a writer and came down here because I'm going to do a historical novel about this area. My wife came along to keep me company."

"She does not work?" he asked.

"Oh, yes," I said. "But we—that is, she is going to have a baby."

Zoya kicked me beneath the table but that was her only reaction.

"Congratulations," he said heavily. "I would not have guessed she was so far along."

"She's still only in the first few months," I said. "She hardly shows yet. But she has not been feeling well since it started, and the doctor suggested to the union that she stop work until after the baby is born."

"New Soviet citizens are important," he said. "What did you say your name was?"

"Yuri Marshak, and this is my wife, Natasha," I said. "I am not a very important writer. You probably have never heard of me."

"Yes, I think I recall the name," he said thoughtfully. "I try to read as much as I can, but the press of duties, you know. ... But I'm sure I remember your name from something I've read." His manner had become much more friendly.

He was as big a phony as I was. He'd probably never read a book in his life, but he wasn't going to admit it. That was what I had gambled on when I decided to say I was a writer.

"May we have the honor of offering you a drink, sir?" I asked again.

He nodded. "Yes, I will join you in a drink to your future

citizen of the Soviet Union," he said. "I am Colonel Kotr Antonovich, of the Ministry of Internal Affairs in Stalingrad."

"I am honored," I murmured. I snapped my fingers for a waiter and this time one came running quickly. He must have noticed that the Colonel and I had become friendly.

I ordered vodka for all of us. I wanted the Colonel to get as much as he could hold—and then a little more.

Our vodka came and, as we drank, we continued to talk. Mostly about general subjects. I was thankful that they were all things which I knew something about. Once in a while something would come up that I knew nothing about, but each time Zoya came to my aid. If I hesitated for even a split second, she would step in with a comment that would pull me out.

I ordered more drinks when those were gone, and after that the Colonel insisted on buying us a drink. His speech was already getting a little thick. I wasn't too far from it myself, so I knew something had to happen soon.

"Too bad," I said, "that we don't know of some nice little café where we can all go sit and drink and talk. These hotel dining rooms are too big, like barns. Now, if we were only in Moscow ..."

"Or in Stalingrad," he said. He glanced at his watch. "As a matter of fact, I do know of a café here in Kamenskaya. Perhaps we could go for an hour or two."

"Great," I said. I signaled to the waiter for a check. "I always like the small places where people can sit around and talk like friends."

"So do I," the Colonel agreed. "But what about your wife? In her condition "

"Best thing for her," I said. "I keep telling her to drink plenty of vodka and she will bear me a son who is a real Russian."

"True, true," he said laughing.

The waiter arrived with our bills and we both paid. Then we got up and walked out, arm in arm. When we reached the lobby the Colonel stopped to tell the clerk that if any of his men came looking for him to have them wait until he returned. With that, we went on out to the Zis parked in front.

He was drunk, all right. Several times I thought the Zis was going to go right up on the sidewalk and crash into a store, but each time he got it straightened out at the last minute and we careened on down the street. After ten or twelve blocks of this, which seemed like a hundred, we jerked to a stop in front of a small café with smoky windows.

"This looks like the kind of place," I said with delight. "I have been looking without any luck since we arrived here."

"A lieutenant on my staff in Stalingrad," he said, "once had the misfortune to be stationed here. When he learned that I was coming here, he told me about it."

"That is true loyalty," I said as we got out and started into the café.

"Oh, he is loyal, my lieutenant," the Colonel said. "When he knows that I am lonely, he sends his wife to cheer me up."

It was impossible to be certain, but I had an idea it was a pointed remark. I'd noticed that as the Colonel got drunker, his glances at Zoya had gotten warmer.

We entered the café and a short, fat man rushed up to greet the Colonel. "The usual, sir?" he asked.

"The usual," the Colonel said.

The fat man led us through the café to the back and threw open a door. There was a small private room there with one table and several chairs. There was even a couch against the wall.

"Bring us glasses and a bottle of vodka," the Colonel ordered. "Oh," he said to me, "I just realized that we became so busy drinking to your unborn son that you and your wife never got your dinner. Would you like to order something here?"

"Who needs food when there is vodka?" I said, with a wave of my hand. I was pretending to be drunker than I was, but it didn't take much acting talent.

"A true Russian," the Colonel said, slapping me on the back.

We went in and sat at the table. A minute later the fat man bustled in with three glasses and a bottle of vodka. "Is there anything else you desire, sir?" he asked.

"If there is, we'll let you know," the Colonel said shortly.

The fat man took the hint and went out, closing the door.

"I always use this private room when I come here," the Colonel said as he started pouring generous portions of vodka. "It is so much better than drinking out there, where all the curious can stare at you."

I noticed that he'd maneuvered us when we were sitting down so that he was in between Zoya and me. That was all right. He wouldn't get the chance to make too many passes; too much more of that vodka and I wouldn't be able to do anything about getting us away.

He'd splashed plenty of vodka into all the glasses and now he shoved them at us. "We've been drinking all the toasts to your son. Now let us drink to your beautiful wife."

We drank. He emptied his glass, but I left about an eighth of an inch in the bottom of my glass. In the meantime, I'd gotten one of the little pills from my pocket and slowly managed to crush it in my fingers. The Colonel was busy talking to Zoya, so I picked up my own glass and dropped the fragments in. I held the glass in my hand and swirled it around gentle until they were dissolved in the vodka.

I stood up and reached across the table gathering up Zoya's and the Colonel's glasses and the bottle. "Time we had another little drink," I said thickly. "Besides, I want to make a toast, too."

I poured the glasses full of vodka and set the bottle down with a thump. I pushed Zoya's glass over to her. Then I handed the glass that had been mine to the Colonel. "Got to make a toast," I muttered, lifting my glass.

The Colonel looked at me and waited. There was a gleam of pleasure on his drunken face because he thought I was drunker than he was. He was wrong, but not wrong enough to please me.

"Well," he said finally, "what's your toast?"

"Oh, yes, a toast," I said. "To—to—my beautiful wife." I giggled and drank. Over the rim of my glass, I watched the Colonel empty his. He put the glass down with a thump. There was nothing in his expression to show that he had tasted anything unusual about his drink.

"Colonel," I said, sitting down, "you're a real hero of the

Soviet Union. Tell us how you're going to catch those two spies."

"The two spies," he said. He'd forgotten all about that project for the moment. "Oh, yes. There's nothing to it, my dear." I'd asked the question, but he was answering Zoya. "We know just about where they are. I have given my men a plan, and right now you can be sure they are being surrounded. There may be someone waiting for me at the hotel right now with news that they've been captured."

"That would be wonderful," I said. "Maybe I could run over to the hotel and find out if there is any news for you."

He liked that. He turned to look at me and blinked heavily as he tried to get his eyes into focus. "That's a good idea," he said. His speech was getting much thicker. The pill was working. "You could drive over in my car and I could give you a note. If one of my men is there—is there, it will authorize him to tell you. I could—do—something—"

The last word was hardly recognizable. I think at that moment he also realized what had happened to him. There was some kind of awareness in his eyes and it seemed to me that he was trying to fight the unconsciousness that crept over him. His mouth worked convulsively, but no sound came out. Then his face smoothed out and his head flopped forward. His shoulders and chest followed as he fell forward on the table.

"What happened?" Zoya asked. She looked at me. "Is that what happened to me?"

"Yes," I said. "Help me to get him over on the couch." He was heavy, but we managed to half drag and half carry him to the couch and then straightened him out on it.

"Only proper that you should put him on the couch," I said solemnly. "That's where he was trying to get you. And in your delicate condition, too."

"I know," she said giggling. "I was wondering what you were going to do. I thought maybe you wanted me to ... do what he wanted. A KGB man would have wanted me to in a similar situation."

"But I don't believe in sharing the wealth," I told her. I bent over the Colonel and went through his pockets. There were only two things I wanted. One was the keys to the Zis and the other was his identification papers. I took them.

"He'll certainly guess what happened to him when he wakes up," I said. "In fact, I think he guessed just before he keeled over. So let's make him a present of our identification papers. We shouldn't be carrying them around now anyway."

She handed me hers and I put both of them in the Colonel's pocket and smoothed out his clothes.

"You'll have to go without papers for the time," I said to her, "but I think it'll be all right as long as you're with a colonel of the MVD."

"I suppose so," she said. "How long will he be like that?"

"A good ten hours, at least," I said. "Let's go."

I went to the door and opened it. Before we could step out, the fat man had hurried up. "There is something you desire?" he panted.

"No," I said. "I'm afraid the Colonel has gone to sleep, so we are leaving." I stepped to one side so he could look into the room. The Colonel's mouth had fallen open and he was snoring heavily. "When he awakens, you may tell him that we will meet him at the usual place tomorrow."

"At the usual place? Yes, sir."

"And I'd like to pay you for the bottle of vodka we had," I continued, pulling money from my pocket.

The fat man eyed the money wistfully, but shook his head. "For the Colonel it is on the house. For the Colonel it is always on the house." He didn't sound happy about it, but he was afraid to have it any other way.

"Very well. Don't forget to give our message to the Colonel when he awakens.

Dobroy nochi."

"*Dobroy nochi,*" he said unhappily. He was closing the door gently as we left.

I helped Zoya into the Zis and went around and slid under the wheel.

Zoya giggled. "Milo, I'm drunk," she said.

"I'd hate to have to take a sobriety test myself," I said. I leaned over and kissed her. "But we've got to get over it and get going. Do you think we can still get our clothes back or will the store still be open?"

"It may be," she said.

I turned the key and started the motor. It had a sweet sound. I put it in gear and we started down the street. I was trying to remember the way we'd come and thought I would retrace our route.

"That store," I said, "was right across the street from the hotel and I don't think we'd better drive up there in this car. I'll try to hit the first street this side of that one, in back of the store, and you can walk around and get the clothes."

"All right," she said.

I drove slowly, watching for landmarks. But I overshot my mark. The first thing I knew, I'd reached the street the hotel was on. I quickly made a U-turn and drove back to the next cross street. I drove down it until I thought I was about opposite the hotel, then pulled to the curb.

"Okay, honey," I said. "Go get the clothes. Do you think there might be anyplace you could buy some milk?"

"Milk?" she asked, startled. "Why?"

"I want some," I said. "At least a quart, so if you want any for yourself, buy more than that." I handed her a wad of money. "And be careful."

She stepped out of the car and walked uncertainly away. She was stoned. I hoped she'd be able to be careful.

While she was gone, I started looking through the car. I hit the jackpot at once. In a pocket on the driver's side there was a loaded gun and three extra clips of bullets. It made me feel better just to know it was there. The rest of the car turned up nothing of special interest. There were some cigarettes, a bottle of vodka, a smaller bottle of brandy, and a flashlight. I got out and checked the gas tank. It was oversize, probably holding thirty gallons or more. It was full.

I lit a cigarette and waited, keeping an eye out for any approaching MVD men. A couple of people did come along the street, but the minute they caught sight of the Zis, they crossed over to the other side of the street and hurried away.

A few minutes later Zoya came back, her arms full. I opened the door for her.

"She was still open," she said, climbing in. "She runs a

little dairy store and I was able to get you some milk. But it's goat milk."

"Right now," I said, "I wouldn't care if it were yak milk. Give it to me."

She separated a little tin bucket from the packages. "I had to buy the bucket so I would have something to carry it in."

"That's all right," I said. I took the bucket and removed the lid. I lifted it to my mouth and drank. There was a strong taste to the milk, but it was reasonably cold and I drank it greedily, not stopping until I had finished the last of it.

Zoya had been watching in amazement. "Is that some American custom?" she asked.

"No, just a March custom," I said. "It'll help me sober up, and also I won't feel quite as bad when I do."

"Oh," she said. "I also bought us some bread and cheese. I thought it might help to sober us up. Then if we're going to be up all night, we might get hungry. Is it all right?"

"A good idea," I said. I tossed the empty bucket into the back seat and started the motor. "But we'd better get started."

"Where?"

"Toward Rostov," I said, pulling away from the curb. "I'm sure there's a roadblock at the edge of town, but they ought to let this car through without any trouble."

"What if they stop us?"

"If they even try, I will roar at them. But I think the sight of the car, plus the outlines of a man and woman inside, will do the trick. I'm sure they wouldn't dare shine a flashlight on the Colonel when he's out with a girl. Right now our problem is how to find the road to Rostov."

We drove slowly along until I found what seemed to be the main street. I followed it until I finally saw a sign that indicated Rostov was straight ahead.

We reached the edge of the city, and there straight ahead was the roadblock. Again a fence had been built across the road, with a crude gate in the center. A dozen or more armed men stood in front. All of them leaped to the alert, with guns up, as they saw the car coming toward them. Trying to think what the Colonel might do, I gave them a couple of blasts on the horn. This confused them slightly, but that was all.

I waited until almost the last minute to brake the car. Then I gave them another blast on the horn. One of them, an officer, stepped forward, a gun in one hand and a flashlight in the other. But he was peering at the car as he came. Then, suddenly, when he was still ten feet away, he must have recognized it, for he leaped back as if he'd been about to step on a snake. He snapped a salute at the car and screamed an order to his men at the same time. Several of the men jumped to open the gate.

When it was open, I put the car in gear and stepped on the gas. As we surged through, all the men were drawn stiffly at attention, saluting.

"It is only at times like this," I said, "that I become fond of policemen and soldiers. Their discipline comes in handy."

Zoya giggled. "Want some bread and cheese?" she asked.

"All right," I said.

She broke off a hunk of black bread and another hunk of cheese and handed them to me. I put one hunk in my lap and nibbled on the other; then I'd switch them. It was pretty good.

"By my rough calculations," I said, "we should be about one hundred and thirty-five miles from Rostov. This is a pretty good car, so we should make it in two and a half hours. That will put us there at about two-thirty in the morning."

"What if there are more roadblocks?" she asked through a mouthful of bread and cheese.

"I don't think there will be. They're pretty certain they have us bottled up between Markovka and Kamenskaya, so I doubt if they have set up other roadblocks. If they have, this car ought to get us through just as it did now."

"But for how long?" she asked. "And through how many roadblocks?"

"Enough, baby, I hope," I said. "All you have to do is lead a clean American life and say the name of John Foster Dulles with the proper reverence every morning before breakfast."

"What?" she asked, puzzled.

"A private joke, honey," I said. "Seriously, I think we've got a little time, even though it probably isn't enough to get us out of the country. But nothing will be discovered right away. The Colonel, I'd guess, is quite a drinker and quite a wencher. So, probably, none of his men will think there was anything strange about him driving out of town with a girl. They may be annoyed because he isn't there to give them orders, but they'll carry on so he won't scream at them when he returns."

"What about the café?"

"The owner is going to be unhappy when the Colonel doesn't wake up, but you can safely bet that he won't have the nerve to wake him up. He'll be equally afraid to go looking for someone to report the Colonel's presence. So he'll probably just lock up and wait for the Colonel to come around. That may happen around nine o'clock in the morning. If we could depend on that much time, we could certainly reach the Black Sea and get pretty damn close to Batumi."

"You don't sound as if you thought we'd have that much time," she said.

"I don't," I admitted. "I'll tell you how I think it'll go. The next man in charge is probably the Captain we saw in the hotel dining room. He's not going to stick his neck out very far. And he didn't look like a fool. By this time he probably knows that we're not somewhere between Kamenskaya and Markovka. He may have even found our car. I think he'll accept the idea that the Colonel went off with a girl, but I doubt that he'll be willing to wait until tomorrow morning. It's very possible that he also knows about the Colonel's favorite café. So I think that sometime this morning—maybe by two o'clock, maybe not until three or four—he will go to the café and try to find out who the girl is. That's what I'd do if I were him. Because the Colonel might be angry for being pulled out of bed with a girl, he'd probably be a lot angrier if anything went wrong with this."

"So he'll find out at the café?"

"Yes. He'll find the Colonel and discover he can't be awakened. The café owner will tell him about the couple who was with the Colonel. The Captain will tie it in with the couple who went in the Zis and come up with the right guess. He'll get the Colonel to the hospital and send out an alarm. Then, when the Colonel is brought out of it, things will really start popping, as we say in America."

"Three or four o'clock?" she asked.

"I would say, somewhere between three and six in the morning," I said. "After that, this car will be hotter than a tin pistol and they'll probably have a solid wall of MVD men and Red Army men stretched between us and any border."

I'm sorry, Milo," she said. "It might have been better for you if you hadn't tried to take me with you."

"Don't kid yourself, honey," I said. "They want you, all right, but not nearly as bad as they want me. If they can grab an American Army officer inside their border, they've got a billion dollars' worth of propaganda, and they know it. You not only have *not* made it worse for me; you've helped a hell of a lot. I doubt if I could have gotten away with the trick on the Colonel without you. Chin up, honey. We'll still make it somehow."

"What about the morning?"

"I don't know yet. We won't stop in Rostov. We'll keep on going. With this car, probably no one will think that it's strange that we're driving late at night—not until after the alarm has gone out. If we get to Rostov about two-thirty, say it takes about a half hour to drive through the city, then it ought to take us about three hours to reach Krapotkin. That would make it six in the morning. So let's say we have a fighting chance to reach Krapotkin, although we might get stopped in Kushchevskaya. If we do get to Krapotkin, it'll be only a hundred and twenty-five miles to Novorossiysk and the Black Sea. Maybe we can make a running fight for it. Or if we have to, maybe we can even walk through the fields at night."

"And if we get to the Black Sea," she said, "we still have to find a way to get across it to Turkey."

"True," I admitted. "But there must be somebody there corrupt enough to take us across or sell us his boat. I still have money. If not, then I'll steal a boat."

"Do you know how to run a boat?"

"No," I said cheerfully. "But once in Berlin I took over a Red plane and I didn't know how to fly it either."*

"You never give up, do you?" she asked.

"There's no percentage to it," I said. "Anyway, I'm in a hurry to get back to New York and my business. I'm losing money every day I'm away. Besides, I haven't had a decent martini since I left."

She leaned over and kissed me on the cheek. After that she curled up and went to sleep. I lit a cigarette and concentrated on my driving, pushing the big Zis along about as fast as it would go on those roads.

It was just two-thirty when we hit the city limits of Rostov. It's a big city, with almost a half million people, and there was still some activity in it. Twice I passed policemen who glanced at the car and then saluted. We were in the middle of the city when Zoya awakened. We were both sober by this time.

"Milo," she said, "I'm sorry I sounded so defeated before. I feel better now. I will help you all I can."

"I know you will."

"In fact," she said, "if we do get to Novorossiysk, I know somebody who will help us at least to the extent of hiding us while we try to get a boat."

"Who?"

---

* See *No Grave for March*.

"My brother. Dimitri Aristov. I have not seen him in several years. He works there in the cement industry."

"You're sure he will help?"

"Of course. He is my brother."

I didn't feel as confident as she did that that was a good reason to expect help from him, but I didn't say any more. There might not be any choice about the matter when we got there anyway.

We got on the wrong street in Rostov a couple of times, but we finally hit the right one, and it was only a few minutes past three when we finally left the city limits. I pushed the Zis to its top speed again.

I took some more of the bread and cheese and ate it as I drove, washing it down with some of the vodka. Zoya also ate, but refused the vodka. She still had a slight hangover from our session with the Colonel.

It was a fairly good road and we could hold a consistent speed. It was strange to drive mile after mile and never see a single car, but it was also soothing in a way. If there had been other cars on the road, I would have had to worry about every one of them.

We reached Kushchevskaya about four-thirty in the morning. I tensed up when we reached it, expecting to find anything. But all I saw was a quiet little city without a single light showing or a single person on the street. We swept through it, feeling as if we were driving through a ghost town.

The sky began to lighten before we reached Krapotkin, and by the time we reached the city it was a few minutes past six. The streets were filled with people going to work. By this time

I was certain there had to be an alarm out. I slowed down and pulled the gun from the pocket beside me. I checked it quickly to make sure it was ready to fire.

Nobody paid any attention to us until we reached the center of the town. There at a street intersection there was a police booth with an MVD man standing in front of it. He glanced at us casually, then did a double take.

He grabbed a whistle with one hand and blew a sharp blast on it. With the other, he pulled a gun from the holster at his side.

ELEVEN

There wasn't time just to make a run for it. I still wasn't up even with the police booth and I still had to pass it. It was too close a range. If he was any kind of shot at all, he couldn't help but hit us.

"Grab the steering wheel and hold it steady," I told Zoya. Knowing that she would, I let go of it without even looking. With my left hand I quickly rolled down the window on my side, while I picked the gun from my lap with the other.

He was already raising his gun. There was no time for me to do any fancy shooting. I just aimed the gun at his body and pulled the trigger. I was too close to miss, too. I saw the tunic of his uniform jump a little, then he spun around, his gun going off, and fell. That was all I needed to see. I dropped the gun back in my lap, grabbed the steering wheel and stepped on the accelerator. The Zis leaped forward. As we rushed past the police booth I caught a glimpse of another man inside.

"Well, they know about us," I said, "and in a minute I guess they'll know more about us."

"Did—did you kill him?" she asked.

"I don't know. I don't think so. It looked to me as if the bullet caught him low on the right shoulder, but there's no way I can be certain. There wasn't enough time."

Fortunately there wasn't much traffic on the street. I weaved around startled drivers, pushing the Zis as fast as it would go. It didn't leave me much time for watching for road signs. I told Zoya to watch for the road to Novorossiysk.

The next thing I knew, we were at the edge of the city. There ahead, at the narrowest point of the road, there were several cars drawn across the road, completely blocking it. They had learned their lesson about fences. At the same time I saw a sign that said this was the road to Labinskaya.

Cursing, I threw all my weight on the brakes. The big car bucked and the tires protested as we skidded to a stop. I quickly reversed, spun the car around, and started back the way we had come.

"What's wrong?" Zoya asked.

"Wrong road," I said. In the rearview mirror I could see men piling into the cars and getting them started. I drove fast, but this time I kept a careful watch. Anybody else on the road had to get out of the way on his own. A couple of them almost didn't make it and lost a fender. But finally within a few blocks I saw a sign pointing to the left as the direction for Krasnodar. That was on the way to Novorossiysk, so I turned into the street. The minute I hit it, I shoved the accelerator to the floor.

It was about eight blocks to the edge of the city. I hit the last block at top speed—and there ahead of me there was a Red Army tank across the road, its turret gun pointing directly at me. The barrel was a little high, but it started swinging down as I came into sight. At one side of the tank there was some kind of warehouse, almost flush with the street. There were no more than three or four feet between it and the tank. On the other side there was a little white house with a pretty picket fence around the front yard which was about two feet from the tank.

There wasn't much time and less choice. "Hang on, honey," I said. "This is going to be rough."

Without slackening speed, I spun the steering wheel and hit the picket fence. Just in time, too. The sound of splintering wood was drowned in the belching of the turret gun, shooting at the spot where I had been only seconds before.

The car bounced across the lawn, scraping against a tree, and hit the fence on the opposite side of the yard. The wooden pickets flew through the air and then we were in a field beyond the house. There was a deep ditch between the field and the road, but farther ahead I noticed there was a spot where the ditch had been filled in making an entrance to the field.

The field was even rougher than the lawn and it was all I could do to hang on to the steering wheel. The rough terrain had also slowed the car down considerably. But my only worry was the tires; if they held up, we might make it.

We reached the spot. I shifted into second gear and pushed the accelerator down.

The wheels spun on the grass, then we were across on the road again. I would have liked to stop to look at the tires, but there certainly was no time for that.

Behind us, the tank was trying to move out of the way of the following cars, and its turret was also swinging around to bear down on me again. I shifted back into high and the Zis lunged ahead.

I kept an eye on the rearview mirror and breathed a sigh of relief when I realized I would be out of range by the time the turret gun was lined up. They tried it anyway but the shot was about fifty yards short. In the meantime, the tank was out of the way and the other cars were speeding in pursuit.

The car in front was certainly a Zis and it was probable that the others were, too. That meant that they would be as fast as the car I was driving. They probably couldn't gain on me, but neither could I get any farther away from them. At least they were far enough behind me to make any attempts to shoot me fairly futile. They did fire a few times, but then must have realized the futility themselves, for they stopped. I turned all of my attention to the problems ahead of me. One of them was just the driving in order to make sure they didn't gain.

"Light me a cigarette, honey," I said. "Problems, problems …"

She lit a cigarette and put it between my lips. "Which one of our problems?" she asked lightly, but I could hear the tension in her voice.

"All of them," I said, "but one at a time. Do you know this part of the country at all?"

"No."

"That makes us equal," I said. "All I know about it I learned from a map before I came here. I know that we have about one hundred and twenty-five miles to go before we hit Novorossiysk—and I think we have just about enough gas to make it. Now, they're certainly going to phone ahead to have a whole army out to block us somewhere. I imagine the logical place will be at Krasnodar, although I suppose it might be anywhere. Now, we might have a better chance of ducking around the next roadblock if those jokers behind weren't so close. I can't shake them with speed, and they're too close for any experimenting. We don't dare let them get close enough for any accurate shooting, which means we have to hold the lead we have now."

"So what will you do?" she asked.

"There might be a small chance if Krasnodar is the next place they try to stop us. I can't be sure since all I saw was a map, but the road around there looks to be twisting, and we'll be out of sight of them for a few seconds occasionally. And there is some sort of road branching off from this one just before we hit Krasnodar. It rims along the Kuban River to Krimskaya, also on the Black Sea to the north. It is also a winding road. Maybe if we take that, we'll have a chance to duck off and they'll go on, thinking we are going to Krimskaya. Then maybe we can find a way to go around Krasnodar and get on this road beyond the roadblock."

"I'm sorry I cannot help any," she said.

"There are too many maybes," I said. "But we don't have much choice. Even if we could crash straight through any roadblock they've set up, the following cars would still be right behind us when we reached Novorossiysk and we wouldn't have a chance to ditch the car and find your brother. We certainly can't go running up to his house with a whole bunch of cops on our tail."

"We'll do whatever you think best," she said. "I can shoot, too, you know. I was taught by the KGB."

Okay, honey," I said. I was beginning to feel the tiredness in my shoulders. I had driven about three hundred miles, most of it at top speed, without a rest. "Get out the vodka bottle and pour some of it into me."

She took the bottle from the compartment, opened it, and put it to my mouth and tilted it. When I'd had enough, I grunted and she took it away.

"Another cigarette," I said.

She lit one and put it in my mouth. The vodka burning in my stomach and the cigarette in my mouth gave me the illusion of feeling better.

I watched the mileage on the speedometer, and when I knew we were getting near to Krasnodar, I began to try to pick up a little extra lead. I did it by taking chances, not losing speed on the curves. A couple of times we almost didn't make the curve. I might not have done it except that we hadn't met a single car coming the other way, so there was little chance of a head-on collision. But it seemed to me that I was gaining a few extra yards. There were also enough curves by this time so that at least half of the time we were out of sight of the pursuing cars.

Finally we came in sight of a city that had to be Krasnodar. Just before it, I could see the river curving away to the north and the little road that followed it. I was glad to see that it seemed to be as winding as it had appeared on the map. Looking back, I estimated I had picked up an extra hundred yards' lead.

I took the turn at full speed, the car skidding dangerously but staying on the road. I had to cut the speed in order to make the curves on the new road, but I knew our pursuers would too. They had been able to see me take the turn and so they were still following.

I watched the side of the road carefully as we whirled around curve after curve. We'd gone about a half mile when we rounded a curve and I saw what I was looking for. A rough wagon road, with grass growing between the two tracks, led off to the left, passing behind a ramshackle building that looked as if it had once been a barn. I braked as fast as I could and turned off. The ground was hard enough not to leave any tire marks. I swung the Zis in behind the building and cut off the motor. I picked up the gun and waited. If this didn't work, it was going to be a rough day.

A moment later we heard the roar of the other motors. They swept up even with us, then snarled on past without slackening. I listened as they started to fade, and held my breath. The big gamble was what was around the next curve. If there just happened to be a long stretch of road, we'd be dead ducks because they'd know we'd turned off here. But the motors continued to fade away with no hesitation in the even tenor of their song.

Only when they had completely faded did I relax and let out the breath I had been holding. I dropped the gun back into my lap and lit a cigarette. "Well, it's working so far."

"For how long?"

"No way of saying for sure," I said. "With any kind of luck, they shouldn't be certain they have been tricked for about a half hour. Then it will take them another half hour to get back here. So say we have an hour, give or take fifteen or twenty minutes. It might be enough. Anyway, it's more time than we've had since we hit Krapotkin."

I started the motor and began driving slowly along the wagon road.

"Where does this go?" she asked.

"I haven't the faintest idea," I said. "But it must go someplace. In the meantime, it's in the direction we want to go and it avoids Krasnodar—and that we must do at all costs. If this turns out to be a dead end and if we have to abandon the car and walk the rest of the way, it's still better than trying to go back and go through Krasnodar. They've had plenty of time here to back up any roadblock, and we'd probably never get through."

We bumped along over the rough road for almost three miles without seeing anything except a herd of cows. And then we topped a small hill to come suddenly upon what looked at first glance like a small village. Our little wagon road ended at a big iron gate, but beyond it and the buildings I could see what looked like a better road winding on through the fields.

"What's this?" I asked.

"I think it's a collective farm," Zoya said. "There are several of them in this area."

I brought the Zis to a stop in front of the big gate and gave a long blast on the horn. Nobody showed up, so I hit the horn again. Finally a little sour-faced man showed up and looked at us through the gate.

I rolled down my window and stuck my head out. "Where does that road go?" I demanded, pointing to the private road beyond the buildings.

"Krasnodar," he said. "Where else could it go?"

"Does it come out in Krasnodar? Or does it hit the highway this side of Krasnodar?"

"About a mile this side of Krasnodar. But it is still much shorter than the old way."

"All right," I snapped. "I'm Colonel Antonovich of the Ministry of Internal Affairs. Open the gate and let me through."

"It's a private road," he said uncertainly. "It belongs to the Collective."

"I don't care if it's a bedroom," I said. "I'm using it. Open the gate."

"Perhaps the director—" he began.

I didn't want him calling the director of the farm; he might have heard enough of the news to guess the rest. "Tell your director to get in touch with the MVD if he wants to make a complaint," I said. "Now open the gate. We're in a hurry."

The voice of authority was too much for him. He unfastened the gate and swung it open.

"Why did you come along the old road?" he grumbled. "Nobody uses it anymore."

"Because we came from that direction," I snapped. He had the gate open by that time. I put the car in gear and drove through. I drove slowly as we made our way among the houses and buildings, but as soon as we were beyond them, I opened the car up as much as was safe on the road.

It was no more than a half mile to the highway and we were soon there. We could see Krasnodar about a mile away off to the left. Then, as we pulled into the road, we could also see the roadblock that had been set up at the very edge of the city. It was too far to tell exactly, but it looked as if they had at least three tanks and several cars as well as several men. Up to one side there was something that looked like a machine-gun placement.

I turned to the right and the Zis began to pick up speed. I kept looking in the rearview mirror. Just as we reached the first curve, I saw one of the cars start moving in our direction.

"They spotted the car and they're sending someone to check on it," I said to Zoya. "But he's a good mile and a half behind us and won't be able to close it."

"But they'll telephone ahead."

"Oh, yes, Novorossiysk will be alerted, but that we have to expect. We've got about an hour before we reach Novorossiysk. Try to rest, if you can. We'll need all our strength when we get there."

She obediently curled up on the seat and closed her eyes.

I kept the Zis at top speed. Every once in a while I would get a glimpse of the car behind, but it never managed to get any nearer. Just before we reached Novorossiysk, the road began to climb over the edge of the mountain range. I knew from the map that the road would cross this tail of the mountain, which wouldn't get very high, then drop down to sea level, then a short distance to the left we'd find Novorossiysk where it nestled between the mountain and the Black Sea.

When we reached the highest spot on the road, I stopped to look. I could see part of the city at the edge of the sea, although I couldn't see most of the road leading to it. On our left the heavily wooded mountain went up at a gradual rate;

on the right there was a sharp drop with only a small wooden barrier to keep cars from going over it.

I looked behind us. Because of the angle of the road and curves, I could only see the other car occasionally. But it would soon be up with us. I awakened Zoya and she climbed out of the car. I put the gun away in my pocket, put the car into low gear, and headed it directly for the wooden barrier. Just before it got there, I jumped out.

The car hit the fence, bucked for a minute, then the wood gave way with a splintering sound and the car went over. The last we saw of it were the two spinning rear wheels. Several seconds went by before there was a tremendous crash from below. I went over and looked. It was a broken heap about a thousand feet down. Flames were already starting to spring up from it.

"Now, up into the woods," I said to Zoya, "and quickly."

We ran across the road and into the woods. It was a fairly steep climb, but we continued to run. We were two or three hundred yards into the woods when I heard the other car stopping down below. I reached out and touched Zoya and she stopped. The motor of the car was still running, so we couldn't make out anything that was being said, although we could hear the murmur of two or three voices. After a bit the motor was cut and we heard a voice ordering someone to go down and look.

I motioned to Zoya and we went ahead in the woods, walking carefully so as not to make too much noise. I led the way for about another quarter of a mile.

"All right, we can talk now," I said, "but not too loudly.

It should take them a little time to make sure that we're not down there with the car. It'll take them a little longer to really organize a search party, and by that time we should be out of here."

"How?" she asked bluntly. "Neither of us knows the area."

"True," I admitted, "but soon we'll be right above Novorossiysk. In some respects, I imagine that Russian men and boys are just like the men and boys in other countries. When they have the chance they probably come up into these woods to hunt rabbits and squirrels. If they do that, then there must be paths by which they come and go. So we will keep bearing right as much as we can and keep going until we find such a path."

"All right," she said. "I'm sorry, Milo. I should have known that you had some sort of an idea."

We kept working to the right until finally we were right on the edge of a cliff that went straight down. Then we went along the cliff. We must have walked a mile, maybe a little more, before we came across a path. It went down the steep mountainside at an angle and had obviously been trodden by many feet. In fact, as we started down it, I found an old used shell from some small-bore gun. I put it in my pocket for good luck.

It was a path, all right, but it was steep and the going was rough. A couple of times Zoya almost fell and I caught her just in time; once she grabbed me when my foot slipped on a pebble. It took us almost two hours to make it down the side of the mountain, although the distance was probably less than half a mile.

When we were finally down, we were at the very edge of the city. We crossed a field and then we were on a street. We went several blocks before we came to a store, where Zoya asked directions to reach the street where her brother lived.

It was only a few blocks away and we soon reached it. It was a large apartment house and her brother lived on the third floor. We climbed the stairs and found her brother's apartment. She knocked on the door.

After a minute the door opened and a man stood there. He was considerably older than Zoya, but there was a family resemblance in his face. He glanced at me first, then his gaze went to her. There was no change in his expression.

"You know what has happened?" she asked.

"The whole world knows," he said sourly. "Why have you come here?"

"Because we need help," she said simply.

"I can't help you," he said, shaking his head.

"I don't mean that kind of help," she said. "All we need is a place to spend tonight and tomorrow. Then we'll leave."

There was a stubborn look on his face. "Come inside. We can't talk about it out in the hall."

He turned and went inside and we followed him. We were in an apartment that was much larger and nicer than the average in Russia. It looked to be at least two rooms, maybe three, and there were no signs that it was shared with another family. There was a pretty blonde woman and a little boy of about two in the room we entered.

"Go cook," the man said gruffly to her. "Take Sasha with you."

The woman got up and left without a word, taking the little boy with her. When she was gone, he turned to Zoya again. "I suppose this is the American?"

She nodded.

"How could you get in such a mess?" he asked. "How could you do it to the memory of your mother and father? How could you do it to me? I'm superintendent at the cement works now."

"Look, Dimitri," she said. "I didn't get into any mess. I made a mistake in judgment, but it seems a KGB agent is not permitted that. The American rescued me from prison. Now we're going to leave the country—or were you thinking of calling the police?"

"No," he said quickly. "I suppose it's better if you get away than if you're on trial. So far they haven't bothered me, but I'm sure they'll start being suspicious of me."

"Look," I said, deciding to get into the act, "we don't want to cause you any trouble. I doubt if we can make arrangements to get out of Novorossiysk before tomorrow night, but all we ask is that we stay here tonight. We'll leave early in the morning. In fact, that'll probably be best for everybody."

"What do you mean?"

"So far, they've been busy just chasing us. By now they certainly know that we are in the area of Novorossiysk. By tomorrow morning they will be going through Zoya's dossier to see if she knows anyone here. You can be pretty certain that sometime tomorrow they will be around here. So we'll leave in the morning, and when they come you can just say you haven't see us."

He was still shaking his head, feeling sorry for himself.

"Come, Milo," Zoya said, "we'll find another place to stay."

"No," he said. "It's better that you stay here than that you wander around on the street. I'll let you stay here tonight, but you must know, Zoya, that I'm doing it for the memory of our dead mother."

"Nonsense," I said roughly. "You're doing it because you think maybe you can save your own skin—the same reason we're trying to get away. So don't make any speeches about it. And, incidentally, we'll pay you for the night and for any food we eat."

He glared at me. "In American dollars?"

"If you want them. Or in rubles."

"I'll take rubles," he said shortly. "I will tell my wife you will eat with us." He got up and left the room.

Zoya looked at me. "I'm sorry, Milo," she said.

"It'll be all right, honey," I said. I wasn't so sure of it myself. I thought he might just as easily turn us in if he thought it would do him more good, but there was no point in telling her that.

"All right," he said gruffly, coming back in. "You two can sleep in here tonight. You can leave when I get up to go to work in the morning—which is early." He picked up a paper and started to read. That was the last word he said to either of us that night.

We had a simple but good dinner. All of us together, but there was no conversation. Both his wife and little boy seemed afraid to speak, so he had probably threatened both of them.

Later, when it was dark out, I told Zoya that I was going to see what I could arrange. She would listen for my knock and let me in. She went to the door with me, gave me a kiss, and asked me to be careful. I went out into the night.

It took me a half hour or so to find the docks. Except for the far end where the dock ended, it was well lighted. I also noticed there was a good-sized patrol going back and forth, but they didn't seem to be stopping anyone. Of course, also, no one was trying to leave in any of the boats moored there.

There was a small café at one end of the dock. It was filled with men who looked as if they were fishermen. I went in and found a seat near a group that seemed to be having a good time. I ordered a double shot of vodka. The first chance I had, I got into a conversation with the man nearest me about fishing. I'd been right. They were all fishermen. We talked about fishing for almost an hour, while I bought more vodka, and once included him in the round. He was mostly bragging about how many fish he and his friends had caught.

"Do all the fishermen do as well?" I asked.

"Oh, no," he said. "Many do not do half as well."

"Tell me," I said, "who among you has done the worst this year?"

He laughed. "That would be old Pyotr Ignatov. Many days he comes back empty-handed. He has not caught enough to even give his family fish dinners, to say nothing of selling."

"Is he here tonight?"

"Over there," he said, pointing to a corner where a lone man sat. "Nursing his one beer. Everyone is afraid to sit with him for fear his bad luck is catching."

"It might be fun to hear his excuses," I said. I got up and moved over to the corner. The man who sat there was small and frail-looking. He was probably about sixty, although it was hard to tell because his face was weather-beaten and heavily lined. He looked up in astonishment as I sat down at his table.

I beckoned the waiter and ordered a drink for myself and told him to bring one for the old man. The waiter looked even more astonished. But he trotted off and returned with the two drinks.

"Aren't you afraid of catching my bad luck?" the old man asked when the waiter had gone.

"I'm not a fisherman," I said, "so I don't have to worry about that. They tell me you haven't been catching many fish."

"It's bad," he said. "When I was a boy it would have been said it was evil spirits, and I would have gone to light a candle and then it might have been all right again. But now when you don't catch fish, they call your bad luck a lack of ability. Bah." He spat on the floor.

"Maybe it's your boat," I suggested. "What kind do you have?"

"A motor-driven one," he said. "It is a few years old, but it is in excellent condition. I always take good care of it."

"How large is it?"

"Two people can fish from it, but it is better for one. But it is just as good as the bigger ones. I paid three thousand rubles for it when I bought it. The fishing was good then."

"That is probably the trouble," I said solemnly. "The boat has run out of luck and that is why you do not catch fish."

He looked at me sharply to see if I was making fun of him. "If that is it, there is nothing one can do."

"There might be," I said. "Maybe I can help you."

He looked at me. "How?"

"Suppose I bought your boat from you. This could be an agreement just between the two of us. Then, after I bought the boat, I would steal it. That way you might even get the boat back eventually. And with its bad luck gone."

"So?" he said softly. "You are one of those who would like to take a night trip?"

"If I did what I was thinking about," I said, "I would pay you ten thousand rubles for the boat."

His mouth stayed open for a minute. "You must want to take a trip badly," he said. "Not that I care, you understand. If I were younger I might want to take a trip myself. But I am too old to learn the ways of another country. But if we were to make such a bargain, how would it be arranged? It represents difficulties."

"True," I said. "Neither of us knows the other and there is the matter of trust. But I think we could work it out. Suppose we talk for a minute." I signaled for more drinks and waited until they were served and the waiter gone.

"Do you have to moor your boat in any one spot?"

"No. Wherever there is an empty place."

"Do you think, say tomorrow night, if you wanted to, you could moor your boat at the far end of the dock where there is not much light?"

"If I wanted to."

"And is there any reason why tomorrow night, at a time we agree upon, you couldn't go down and start tuning up the motor? Then walk a few boats away, leaving the motor running, to talk to someone or look at something?"

"It could be done," he said. He squinted at me. "How would you know that there was enough gas to take you anywhere? Or how would you know that I had not told someone about the arrangement?"

"I wouldn't," I said, "but I think that might be fixed, too. Is there someone around here that you trust? Completely?"

"That's a lot to ask," he said with a toothless grin. "But there is. Him." He nodded his head to where a heavyset man with a huge mustache leaned against the wall, watching the waiters scurrying around. "He is the owner of this café. We grew up together as boys. He is a real Russian in the old sense. We are still friends."

"All right," I said. "Suppose tonight I were to give you one thousand rubles. Tomorrow I let your friend see me put nine thousand rubles into an envelope, which I then leave with him. Unless I come back for the envelope by a certain time—or unless a friend of mine comes by the certain time with proof that I am dead or in prison—he will then turn the envelope over to you."

"I can see you are a man of experience," he said. "But what if my friend turns the envelope over to me before the given time?"

"Then," I said pleasantly, "either I or my friend would take steps to see that the circle of justice was completed."

"You are a man of experience," he said. "It sounds all right to me. But how do I know you have that much money? It is a great amount."

"I will give you a thousand tonight. I will be here before noon tomorrow and your friend will see the other nine thousand. So it will be real enough before you have to do anything."

He nodded. "Ten thousand rubles will make up for many fish that got away. I will do it."

"Good," I said. Under the table I counted out a thousand rubles. I passed them to him, still beneath the table, and he counted them the same way.

"Perhaps," I said, "you'd better point me out to your friend so he will know it's all right tomorrow."

"I will be here tomorrow at noon," he said, "and I will signal him then. I will be going out fishing at daylight as usual, but I'll be back at noon."

"All right. Don't get drunk on the thousand rubles and talk too much."

He grinned at me again. "When one is as old as I am, one learns not to talk about certain things. Do not worry."

I nodded and got up. I made my way leisurely through the crowd, stopping briefly beside the man I had first talked to. "You were right," I said. "He is very funny with his tale of bad luck."

"Poor old Pyotr," he said, laughing. "His only bad luck is that he is old, but he will not admit it."

I agreed and left the café. I walked quickly back across town and soon arrived at the apartment house. Just as a precaution I walked past it, looking to see if there was anyone watching the place. There didn't seem to be. I went upstairs and knocked. Zoya opened the door and looked relieved when she saw it was me.

She didn't ask any questions. I didn't say anything until after her brother and his wife went to the other room. Zoya and I went to bed and I whispered the whole story to her.

"I'm frightened, Milo," she said. "Please hold me tightly."

I held her close until the tension left her body and it became soft with desire. Later, we went to sleep with our arms around each other.

It was barely daylight when Zoya's brother awakened us. We got dressed quickly and had breakfast with him. It consisted of some grape juice, a roll each, and coffee. After breakfast, I gave him a hundred rubles and we left.

We wandered across town, stopping in a café for some more coffee. Then we found a motion picture house that was playing some old Soviet movies. They weren't bad pictures and it seemed like a good place to stay. When it was almost noon, I left Zoya there and went to the waterfront again.

There were only a dozen or so customers in the café when I entered. I spotted the old man sitting in the same corner and saw him nod as I entered. I walked up to the man with the mustache and said I'd like to talk to him. He turned and led the way into the back, where there was a small storage room. He handed me an envelope without speaking.

I counted out nine thousand rubles and placed them in the envelope, then sealed it.

"Tell your friend that the hour is seven o'clock tonight," I said. "Now, you understand that if I do not come for this envelope by eight o'clock, or a friend of mine does not come by eight o'clock with proof that I am dead or in prison, then you are to turn it over to your friend Pyotr."

"Yes," he said.

"You also understand," I said, "that it will go bad for both of you if it does not go exactly as I have told you?"

"Yes," he said again. He was evidently not a talkative man.

I gave him the envelope and turned and walked back through the café to the street. I made two stops on the way back to the theater. I bought some black bread and cheese, and I stopped in a government store and bought a small compass and a large box of matches. Then I went on to the theater and slipped back into the seat next to Zoya.

We stayed there all afternoon, munching on bread and cheese when we were hungry. By the time evening came, I knew both of the pictures by heart. We left in time to stop at a café and have some dinner. We each had two vodkas with our meal. Then we set out for the waterfront.

We arrived near the far end of the dock, stopping a block away and surveying the scene. It looked much as it had the night before. The MVD men were still patrolling the dock, and there were a few fishermen strolling around. It was possible that some of them were cops, too. Everything else seemed the same, too.

It was five minutes before seven. Zoya and I stood there, holding hands like two lovers staring out at the Black Sea.

"It won't be long now, honey," I said to her.

A few minutes later I saw the figure of the old man walking down the dock. He went to the last boat on the line and clambered aboard. He fired up the engine, and began fooling with it. That, too, seemed normal, for along the line several men were working on their boats, and I noticed that the MVD men gave him no more than a glance.

Zoya and I began to walk casually down toward the dock. We were almost there when the old man hopped out of his boat and walked down to another boat a few places away. Even before he got there, I heard him calling out to ask the owner if he had a match. Zoya and I quickened our steps.

We had almost reached the boat when I suddenly became aware that four men had appeared from somewhere on our right and were almost up to us. They were running, and I could see the glint of metal in the hand of the man in front.

"Major Milo March," this man said, "please put your hands up quickly. I am most glad to see you." There was a triumphant note in his voice.

There was only one thing to do. I shot him in the stomach. Even while the gun was recoiling I swung on the second man and shot him. By this time the other two men were shooting, but they were hurrying too much. I tried to ignore the sound of the shots and the bullets screaming by. I brought the gun in line on the third man and shot again. He went down. I wasn't trying to be fancy with any of them. I was just aiming for the stomach and letting go. It was the easiest place to hit, and the Colonel's gun was heavy enough to stop any man. The fourth man was close now and firing wildly. He was still running, which was also throwing his aim off. I fired again and he went down.

That was the four of them, but there were still gunshots. I looked around. The MVD men were running down the dock, firing as they ran. About a dozen fishermen were running with them, also shooting. So I'd been right about some of the fishermen being cops. It was quite an army charging down the dock. At least thirty men.

"Come on, honey," I said turning to Zoya. But she wasn't there. Then I saw her. She was on the ground.

There was no time to examine her. I bent and scooped her up in my arms.

"No, Milo," she said. Her voice sounded small and far away. "It's too late. I'm going to die." I looked down at her and saw the bloody froth around her lips and knew it was true. "Perhaps it's better this way. I belong—to Russia. It would—have been nice—to work with you—in America, but—it's—too late. Now—put me down. ..."

I started to tell her I wouldn't when her head fell back and her body went limp. She was right. It was too late. I put her down. I straightened up, snapped a couple of shots at the running men, and dashed to the boat. I knocked the mooring rope off and leaped into the boat, hoping that its controls were not too different from the boats I had known. They weren't. I threw it into reverse and pulled the throttle. It surged backward. I cut the throttle, threw it into forward gear, pulled the throttle, and spun the wheel. The little boat almost stood on its propeller as it spun around and headed away. The motor was drowning out the sound of the shots, but I could see bullets hitting the water around me.

I glanced back, intending to answer their fire, but my attention was caught by something else. Standing farther away under a light there was a familiar figure. He was watching intently. It was Zoya's brother. And suddenly I knew why there had been so many cops at the docks.

It was a long range, but I tried anyway, pulling the trigger three or four times as fast as I could. The figure disappeared, but there was no way of knowing whether I'd hit him or merely scared him so that he'd ducked to the ground.

I had to turn my attention back to the boat because it was weaving wildly. I straightened it out and then began a deliberate zigzag course. I knew some of the MVD men probably had rifles, and I didn't want to be any better a target than I had to.

The bullets continued to dance around me for a few more minutes, but I soon ran out of range. I heard some other motors roar into life back by the dock and knew they were starting a chase, but that didn't worry me too much. I was already well out into the darkness. I checked to be sure that I had no running lights on. They'd have a lot of trouble finding me if they only used the other fishing boats. I crouched down in the boat and got out my compass and matches. I struck a match and looked at the compass. I swung the wheel with one hand until I knew I was headed in the right direction. Since everything was complete darkness, I'd have to check every so often in order to stay on course.

It was when I straightened up that my left shoulder hurt. I struck another match and looked at it. My shirt and coat were soaked in blood. But there didn't seem to be any fresh blood seeping out, so it would just have to wait.

Somewhere behind me the other fishing boats were racing around, but none of them came near and the only lights they had were flashlights. I could see the slender pencils of light stabbing out into the darkness, but they couldn't reach far. And after a while I couldn't see them anymore.

Checking my position frequently, I roared through the night for a little more than an hour when I suddenly became conscious of the beat of powerful motors. I looked around and soon saw the sweep of searchlights. They were still some distance away and I watched them carefully. It was two ships, probably destroyers, working together and making a careful search of the ocean. I watched them for a while and began to see a pattern. Circling around and working in conjunction, they would carefully search a large area of the ocean, then they'd come straight ahead for a distance and repeat the operation. And they were moving steadily toward me. I couldn't possible get enough speed out of the little boat to run away from them.

Once I'd worked out their pattern, I turned my boat and went directly toward them. I swung out to one side and timed it so that I could make an approach while they were on their straight run. Then dodging the long sweeps from the searchlights, I went straight in toward one of the destroyers. There was a little danger in it, but not as much as being at a distance. Once I got near enough to the destroyer, the searchlight couldn't reach me.

They started their circling and I stuck to my one ship. I was far enough from the stern to be safe from the propeller wash, but I had to watch the turns. A couple of times I came within two feet of the sleek black sides, and one little tap would probably have smashed my boat.

When they finally straightened out to move ahead again, I turned and took off in the direction from which they'd come. By the time they started circling again, I was out of reach of the searchlights. I cut the throttle down and waited. Finally, they were far enough away for me to light a match and get my compass bearing again. Once more I set off on course.

From there on, everything seemed to be a giant black void in which I sat with a roaring motor—going nowhere. I checked position every few minutes and usually had to correct it. Twice I saw the searchlights of the destroyers again, but each time they were far away and never came nearer. Then finally I didn't see them anymore and there was nothing but the blackness of the night. Between the unending darkness and the hum of the motor, it was difficult not to go to sleep.

It seemed as if I'd been in that little boat for days when the sky finally began to lighten. About a half hour later, when it was beginning to be pretty light, I saw land ahead. Unless I'd made a big mistake, it was Turkey.

As I drew nearer I was glad to see that I was headed for a long and empty stretch of sandy beach. There was not a single building in sight. A few minutes later I was in shallow water. I stopped the boat and shut off the motor. I took off my socks and shoes and tied them around my neck. I rolled up my pants legs and climbed over the side of the boat. The water was only up to my knees. I pushed the boat around until it was headed out to sea. I used a rope in the bottom of the boat to lash the wheel. Then I started the motor and put it in gear. It pulled slowly away from me. I turned and waded to the shore.

Once ashore, I sat down and took stock. There was a chance that I might be temporarily detained in Turkey. I took the code paper of the CIA and my own identification and put them in the bottom of my socks. Then I put on my shoes. I still had the Colonel's identification. I dug a hole in the sand and buried it. The only thing I had left then were American dollars and

Russian rubles. I kept both of them, putting each kind in a different pocket. Then I started walking across the sand.

I'd walked about a mile when I came to a small farmhouse. There was a fresh wash hanging out on the line. I didn't see anyone around, but I finally approached the house. There wasn't anyone there. The wife, I decided, must be out in the fields with her husband. I went over and took one of the shirts that was hanging on the line. It was almost dry and looked as if it wouldn't be much too big for me. I pinned a five-dollar bill to the line where the shirt had been; then, carrying it, I walked on.

Farther on, I stripped off my bloody coat and shirt and buried them. I looked at my shoulder. It was a little puffy, but didn't look too bad. I put on the clean shirt and made a little inspection of myself. Considering what I'd been through, I looked all right. I needed a shave and my clothes were a little baggy, but I might be able to get by.

I kept on walking until I came to a road and followed it to a small town about three or four miles away. I didn't know exactly where I was, although I knew where I wanted to go. The question was going to be how to get there. I couldn't go in anywhere and change my dollars for Turkish money without showing my passport. Since I didn't have anything permitting me to be in Turkey, that would mean the cops, which I didn't want. I had last been officially in Germany—which was going to be enough of a problem in itself.

I walked down the main street of the little village trying to get an idea when I saw a bus standing at the curb. On the front its destination was announced as Ankara. That was where I wanted to go. I decided to try a small gamble. The driver was sitting in the bus and was all alone. I walked up to him.

"*Merhaba,*" I said haltingly, trying to remember the little Turkish I had once known. "*Ben Amerikanin.*"

"I speak English," he said. He did, too. Better than I spoke Turkish.

So I told him the little story I had just thought up. I said that I'd been down here on a hiking trip and had stayed longer than I had intended so that I had run out of Turkish money and all I had were American dollars. I wanted to get back to Ankara and I wondered if he would either let me pay him in dollars or, when we got to Ankara, come to the Embassy with me and I'd pay him in Turkish money.

He listened solemnly until I was through. "What part of America are you from?" he asked then.

"New York," I said.

"Yeah?" he said with a grin. "I was in New York for five years. You know what I miss the most? Times Square. What I wouldn't give sometimes to be back on Thirty-fourth Street, looking up at all the Times Square lights."

"You mean Forty-second Street, don't you?" I said.

He grinned at me again. "Yeah. I just wanted to see if you knew where it was. Every once in a while we get warned about being careful about Russian spies who sneak over the border. Jump in. You can pay me for the ride in dollars."

"Thanks," I said. I got in and took a seat near him. I figured I had to at least repay him with conversation.

Nobody else got on the bus, and in a few minutes he closed the door and pulled away from the curb. I drew the first really relaxed breath I'd had in days.

TWELVE

The whole two hundred and fifty miles to Ankara was spent in talking about New York City. The driver certainly did miss it. I was bored after the first thirty minutes, but I didn't let him know. Also, by the end of the first thirty minutes we were calling each other by our first names. His was Adnan and he thought mine was Jim because I had given him a phony name. I had an idea that the name Milo March was probably being bandied all over the world.

"Where do you want to go?" Adnan asked when we reached Ankara in the middle of the afternoon.

"I'm going to the American Embassy," I told him.

"We're not as formal here as they are in New York," he said with grin. "I'll drive you there."

And he did. At the entrance to the Embassy we shook hands and I promised to look him up in day or two for a night on the town. He drove off and I went up to the Embassy door.

A nice young man answered the door and managed not to sniff when he got a good look at me.

"I'm an American," I told him, "and I want to see the Ambassador."

"What is your name?" he asked. "And what is your business?"

"I think I'd better tell my name to the Ambassador," I said, "and my business is urgent."

"The Ambassador is busy," he said. "If you'll be more explicit, I'll see if he can see you."

"Look," I said. "I told you my business was urgent and it's too delicate for your young ears. Now, either run in and tell him or I'll push you on the back of your fancy pants and go see him myself."

He sniffed again but went inside, closing the door and leaving me standing outside. But he wasn't gone long. He opened the door. "Follow me," he said stiffly.

I followed him inside and down a long hall. He threw open a door and motioned me inside. He closed the door behind me.

The Ambassador sat at a large desk. There was a stern look on his face. "Now, what is this?" he asked. "Refusing to give your name, threatening Embassy personnel—"

"If you'll wait until I can take a shoe off," I said, "I think you'll understand." I sat down and took my shoe and sock off. I fished around inside the sock until I found my CIA identification. I tossed it on his desk and put my sock and shoe back on. When I looked up, the Ambassador's face was pale.

"Where did you come from?" he asked as if he were afraid of hearing the answer.

"Just between you and me," I said, "from Russia—just as the Russians are saying."

"But Washington has been denying the story," he said weakly.

"Of course," I said, "and it's just possible that we can prove the story false. All I want from you is to use your phone to call West Berlin and then maybe a shower, a shave, some clean clothes, and a drink. Shortly thereafter, I think, you can forget that you ever heard of me."

"But we can't even admit that you're in Turkey," he said.

"I know," I said. "Just let me use the phone and we'll see."

"All right. Use this one. Do you want me to leave the room?"

"Not if you don't care what you hear. Do the Turks listen in on your calls?"

"Probably."

"All right," I said. "We'll keep it safe." I picked up the phone and gave the operator the number I wanted in West Berlin. It was the number at the house where Henri was staying with the Russian.

There followed a lot of conversation between operators in two different languages and finally the phone was ringing on the other end. After a few rings, there was an answer. It was Henri.

"Henri?" I said.

"Ah, my friend," he said happily. "How are you?"

"I'm fine," I said. "How is our mutual friend coming along?"

"Like a lamb. Where are you?"

"Why, in Ankara, Turkey, of course. I'm with my friend the Ambassador." I saw the Ambassador wince at that.

"Of course, I had forgotten," he said. "Have you been keeping up with the news?"

"Oh, yes," I said, "but I haven't yet decided who to bet on the handicap. It looks like a tough course. Why don't you call our friend—the one with stars in his eyes—and see what he thinks. There isn't much time."

"I know," he said. "I'll call you back." The phone clicked

and I hung up, too.

"There'll be a phone call for me from West Berlin sometime soon. He won't ask for me by my real name, of course. You'd better tell your switchboard that if a call comes from there asking for any name that isn't one of your staff to put it through to me." He nodded. "Now, do you suppose I could have that shower and shave?"

He nodded again. He must have pressed a button on his desk, for in a minute the door opened and there was the same young man who had let me in. He looked disappointed as the Ambassador gave him his instructions. But he led me upstairs and showed me a luxurious bathroom. He handed me some shaving equipment and left. I stripped off and got into the shower. It felt good—except for my shoulder. That hurt like hell and was beginning to be an angry red.

I finished my shower and shaved. When I looked out of the bathroom, there were some clothes on the bed. I put them on and they fit fairly well. I started out the door only to meet the same young man again.

"There is a phone call for you," he said. "In the Ambassador's office."

I followed him downstairs to the office. The Ambassador was there. The telephone receiver was lying on the desk. He gestured toward it. "He asked for somebody named Jim Wade."

I picked up the phone and said hello.

"Hello, Jim," Henri said. "It's me again. I think I have some inside information on that handicap, but maybe I can give it to you in person."

"What do you mean?"

"Some of the boys and I are flying over that way and we're going to land at Ankara. We won't have more than an hour, so why don't you and four or five of the boys there come out to the airport and visit with us."

"Fine," I said. I didn't know what he had in mind, but I'd play along. "When will you be here?"

"We're leaving right away. Should be there in less than three hours. Two and a half if the winds are right. By the way, our other friend here wants to know if you found out anything about his rose."

It took me a minute to realize that it was Zoya he was talking about. "The rose completely lost its bloom," I said dully. As I said it, I realized that I'd been suppressing how bad I felt about Zoya. I had known her only a few days, but I'd become close to her in that time—in many ways. "I've lost part of my own bloom since I saw you last."

"Oh?" he said. "Well, none of us is getting any younger. See you soon." He hung up.

I put the receiver back and looked at the Ambassador. "I don't know what the plan is, but I'll have to ask you for one more favor. He's landing at the Ankara airport in about two and a half hours, and he wants me and four or five men from here to come out and visit for an hour."

"I guess it can be done," he said. "They're going to think it odd that I didn't introduce you, but I guess they'll take it in their stride. Would you like that drink now?"

"Very much," I said.

He went to a cabinet and brought out some old brandy. It

was just what I needed. It even made me forget some of the throbbing in my shoulder.

Two hours later, four young men from the Embassy staff and I started for the airport in an Embassy car. When we got there, we had to wait for about twenty minutes before we got a glimpse of a big American jet swooping down on the field. A few minutes later Henri and four American Air Force officers came into the terminal bar where we were waiting and descended upon us. They all acted as if they were old friends of all of us. I think it baffled the young men from the Embassy, but they carried it off very well.

After we'd had a couple of drinks at the bar, one of the officers suggested that we might all like to look at the plane since it was one of the newest. It was soon arranged with the airport officials and the ten of us trooped into the plane.

The minute we were inside, Henri grabbed me and one of the officers and shoved us into the rear of the plane. "There's no time for long introductions," he said. "Major Milo March, Captain Jim Wade. Now the two of you change clothes as quickly as possible."

We did it in record time. Henri had picked him carefully. His uniform fit me almost as well as if it had been made for me. And my borrowed clothes fit him well. After we'd changed, we went back to join the others. The ten of us milled around a little longer, then we all descended to the ground, where we said enthusiastic good-byes to the five men and they walked away.

We then checked out with the airport officials and boarded the plane again. Within a few minutes we were roaring into the sky. As soon as we'd leveled off, Henri came to where I was sitting with another one of the officers. "This is Major Swenson," he said, "who also happens to be a doctor. I gathered that you were wounded."

"Yes," I said. I took off my jacket and shirt, and the Major bent over me. He clucked a few times and went to get his black bag. He gave me a small injection in the shoulder and went to work. The injection wasn't enough to deaden it completely and it hurt like hell while he cleaned it out and bandaged it. When he'd finished, he gave me another injection.

"Penicillin," he said. "Now you ought to sleep. Think I ought to give you a sedative?"

"No," I said. "If anybody has a drink, that's all I need."

"I'll get it," Henri said. He darted forward in the plane and came back with a huge vacuum bottle. "I remembered how well you liked dry martinis," he said. "This is full of them."

"Henri," I said, "I love you." I poured myself a martini and started drinking it. "Now tell me what's going on. Where are we heading and how are we going to fix this?"

"There'll be plenty of time to tell you all about it after you awaken," he said. "Right now I'll just tell you that we're on our way to America. I'm going with you to be part of your alibi. Now, finish your martini and go to sleep. When you awaken, I'll tell you the rest."

I felt tired enough to agree. I finished the martini and Henri went away. I leaned back in the seat and was asleep almost immediately.

I awakened hours later, how many I didn't know. I felt much better, although my shoulder still hurt. I lingered for a minute between being asleep and awake, lulled by the steady roar of the jet motors, until I realized that I was imagining that Zoya was beside me and I would soon open my eyes and see her. Then I forced myself to sit up and open my eyes. Henri must have been watching me, for he bustled over.

"You had a good sleep, *mon vieux*," he said. "Now, would you like coffee or one of your martinis?"

"A martini," I said. "And then coffee. Where are we?"

"Already over America. We shall soon be at our destination." He hurried off and came back with the vacuum bottle. I poured a martini into the cup and began sipping it.

"Where is our destination?"

"Ah, I do not understand this America of yours. It is, I am told, somewhere in—could it be Colorado? Where is that?"

"It could be and it's in the West," I said. "Why are we going to Colorado?"

"I do not know all of it," he said. "I spoke to General Roberts, but we spoke in code and he did not go into details. You know that the Russians are making an issue of your being in their country?"

"Yes."

"They have lodged a protest with the U.N. and are making much propaganda. Your government has, of course, denied that you or any other agent was in Russia. They have been demanding that your government then produce you. It is a production for which the entire world is waiting."

"Great," I said. "What do I do? Come on in a ballet costume and say I've been out dancing?"

"I do not know the details, but I believe the general story

is that I, your old friend in Europe, came to visit you about a week ago and the two of us have been away on a fishing trip in the wilds of your Colorado, where we have not seen a newspaper nor heard a radio broadcast. So we did not know that everyone was looking for you."

"What about the fact that I was in Paris a week ago and in Berlin six days ago?"

"I do not know, but I believe that will no longer be true. Remember, there will be no official record that you were there except on your passport. I believe that something of the sort will also apply to the time of my entry into your country."

I nodded. Something like that just might work. All that my phone service in New York knew, or even my lawyer, was that I was to be away for a week or so.

"How do we get into the wilds of Colorado quickly enough?" I asked.

"There is a spot over which they will fly, and then you and I parachute down."

I groaned. "The things I go through to serve my country."

"It is nothing," Henri said. "You must have made many jumps."

"I never made any," I said, "and I'd be just as happy to leave it at that. And you can just stop sounding so pleased. I suppose you're an old hand at that sort of thing?"

"No, but for a half hour before we left Berlin I practiced by jumping off a chair. It is nothing, *mon vieux.*"

"I might as well let you die happy," I muttered. "What happened to our friend I left in your care?"

"He decided it was wiser not to return to Russia and so I

turned him over to the CIA office. By the way, I have your money, passport, and other papers." He dug them from his pocket and passed them over. "Incidentally, you did get the paper you went after?"

"I got it."

"Good. I told General Roberts as much."

Another half hour passed and one of the Air Force officers came back and helped us into our parachutes. Shortly thereafter they told us to get ready to jump. They gave us a short course in what to do, and we were ready. Then it was time. Henri insisted on going first. I watched him disappear through the jump door and then, on the command of one of the officers, I pushed myself out. I did the proper count and pulled the ring clutched in my hand. There was a sharp jerk under my arms and then I was floating lazily. Off to the left and down, I could see Henri. He glanced up and waved.

We came down in a fairly large field in what seemed to be the middle of a forest. It was obviously high in the mountains. My chute dragged me a few feet before I could collapse the silk, which didn't make my shoulder feel any better.

By the time I got untangled from the chute, a jeep had charged out on the field. A man dressed like a mountain guide got out and came to help us pick up the chutes. He introduced himself as Bill Walen. It took me several minutes to recognize him as someone I had occasionally seen around the CIA offices.

He drove us to a camp about a mile away. It was in complete wilderness. It was generously stocked with everything—including a suitcase full of my things from my apartment in New York. There was also a large variety of fresh fish and several changes of well-worn clothes in my and Henri's sizes. The first thing we had to do was go through various changes of clothes and have our pictures taken holding fish. He took the pictures with a Polaroid camera so that the prints were immediately developed. He had Henri and me write dates and data about the fish on the back of each picture.

Then we packed and drove about twenty miles down the mountain until we came to a general store. There I put in a call to General Roberts in Washington. I played it according to script. I had just seen a paper with a story about everyone looking for me, and what was it all about? The general put on quite an act, too. The result was that he asked if I'd mind getting on a plane at once and coming to Washington. Naturally, I didn't mind.

We made it to Denver in another hour and immediately got a plane to Washington—the three of us.

We were met at the plane by a car and a bright young man who undoubtedly belonged to some department, although he never explained. As soon as we were in the car, he asked to see my passport. I handed it over. He pretended to examine it, but I saw him pull a switch. When he handed it back to me, I examined it. The only difference was that the last trip stamped on it was one I had taken to Italy a couple of years before. He then asked for Henri's passport and pulled the same hanky-panky. When he returned it, Henri looked at it and then grinned at me.

We ended up at one of the buildings occupied by the CIA. There was quite a gathering there. About fifty newspapermen,

General Roberts, George Hillyer, Philip Emerson, somebody from the State Department, a couple of curious Congressmen, a representative from the Soviet Embassy—and us. We were the stars. The man from the State Department gave us the build-up. He painted a touching picture of the reunion between two old buddies—Henri and me—and how we had planned a little fishing trip to get away from it all. He almost waxed poetic when he described the place where we had gotten away from it all, with no newspapers or radio, until finally some other guide had dropped by with a paper. He was eloquent in telling how I dashed for the nearest telephone twenty miles away. Finally he introduced the three of us—the two old buddies and their trusted mountain guide.

The questions were hot and heavy. Henri and I played it mostly ad lib, but I thought we were doing a pretty good job. I even began to enjoy it after a bit. Most of the correspondents were friendly, but there were a few who tried to trip us up. They also asked to see Henri's and my passports. Those were passed around. Somebody even wanted to know about the fish we caught. We passed around the pictures.

Finally, when they seemed to run out of questions, the Soviet representative got up. His name was Yelyutin. I had a feeling from the way he acted that he was probably the KGB man in the Embassy. But he was smooth. He managed to do a great job of apologizing for the mistake the Soviet Union had made, while at the same time he was making it plain that he didn't believe a word we had said. Then he got around to another point. They had reports, he said, that the man who had escaped from Russia had been wounded on the left shoulder. Would there be any objection to having a Soviet doctor from the Embassy examine me? There most certainly was. The State Department man went into the indignity and lack of trust in the suggestion and said, in essence, that no American was going to take his shirt off for a Russian.

Mr. Yelyutin apologized again. This time he included a very friendly apology to me directly. He hoped that I would understand there had been nothing personal about it and that sometime we could meet as friends. He got pretty emotional about the whole thing and climaxed it by putting both hands on my shoulders in a brotherly gesture. Only the hand that went on my left shoulder hit hard and then his fingers dug into the wound.

It hurt like hell. There were black spots in front of my eyes and for a minute I thought I was going to pass out. But I managed some sort of smile and kept my voice from cracking as I answered that there wasn't anything personal in it and I loved him like a brother, too. To prove it, I clapped both of my hands on his shoulders, too. I dug my fingers into his shoulder muscles as hard as I could and he winced. Just to make it good, I also stepped hard on his foot. The Soviet representative grew as pale as I must have been.

That did it more than anything else. Everybody in the room had been watching like a nervous bride at a burlesque show with her husband. You could feel all of them relax after that little display of international friendship. Mr. Yelyutin limped back to his place in the audience. As through a fog, I heard the State Department man saying that the government would gladly transport any of the newspapermen to the camp where

I'd been for a week if they wanted to look. Then I was vaguely aware that they were all filing out, and soon there were just the CIA men, the State Department man, and Henri and me.

"That was a great show, Milo," General Roberts said. He advanced on me, ready to slap me on the back. "I'm proud "

"You touch me," I said through gritted teeth, "and I'll kill you. In the meantime, somebody get me a drink. Quick." I still wasn't sure I wasn't going to pass out.

"What's wrong?" demanded the General.

"He is wounded," Henri said. "That pig of a Russian was squeezing the wound as hard as he could. Get him something to drink."

I'll say this for the General: he could move fast when he wanted to. He opened a cabinet and had a bottle of brandy in my hands before Henri stopped talking. I turned it up and drank until I had to stop to get a breath. Then I began reviving. The brandy had started a fire in my stomach that offset the pain in my shoulder. I twitched back my coat to look at it. The white shirt was getting red all along the shoulder.

"Maybe we'd better get a doctor," General Roberts said.

"Don't be a fool," I snapped at him. "And undo everything you just did? I'll get a private doctor after I get away from here. And that can't be too soon for me." I dug into my pockets and came out with the paper I had brought from Russia. "Here's your little souvenir."

He took it and gazed at it reverently. "I knew you'd do it, Milo, my boy. Although I must say it's an expensive piece of paper. It must have cost us thirty or forty thousand dollars to get this back."

"You get a small refund," I said. "Here's about fourteen hundred dollars and some amount of rubles, which you can count yourself." I threw the money on the desk. "By the way, am I still in the Army?"

"Officially, you were never recalled to active duty," he said. "We fixed that right away."

"Lovely," I said. "One more thing. Just make sure that Henri's vacation, which you also fixed, is extended slightly."

"That can be done."

"Because," I said, "Henri and I are now going to go on a real vacation." I turned on Henri. "But no damn fishing, you understand. This vacation we're going to spend in New York bars. I've got a number of things to forget."

Henri grinned and followed me out of the office. We started our vacation at the nearest bar on the way to the airport. But I was careful not to order any vodka.

ABOUT THE AUTHOR

Kendell Foster Crossen (1910–1981), the only child of Samuel Richard Crossen and Clo Foster Crossen, was born on a farm outside Albany in Athens County, Ohio—a village of some 550 souls in the year of this birth. His ancestors on his mother's side include the 19th-century songwriter Stephen Collins Foster ("Oh! Susanna"); William Allen, founder of Allentown, Pennsylvania; and Ebenezer Foster, one of the Minute Men who sprang to arms at the Lexington alarm in April 1775.

Ken went to Rio Grande College on a football scholarship but stayed only one year. "When I was fairly young, I developed the disgusting habit of reading," says Milo March, and it seems Ken Crossen, too, preferred self-education. He loved literature and poetry; favorite authors included Christopher Marlowe and Robert Service. He also enjoyed participant sports and was a semi-pro fighter in the heavyweight class. He became a practicing magician and had a passion for chess.

After college Ken wrote several one-act plays that were produced in a small Cleveland theater. He worked in steel mills and Fisher Body plants. Then he was employed as an insurance investigator, or "claims adjuster," in Cleveland. But he left the job and returned to the theater, now as a performer: a tumbling clown in the Tom Mix Circus; a comic and carnival barker for a tent show, and an actor in a medicine show.

In 1935, Ken hitchhiked to New York City with a typewriter under his arm, and found work with the WPA Writers' Project, covering cricket for the *New York City Guidebook*. In 1936, he was hired by the Munsey Publishing Company as associate editor of the popular *Detective Fiction Weekly*. The company asked him to come up with a character to compete with The Shadow, and thus was born a unique superhero of pulps, comic books, and radio—The Green Lama, an American mystic trained in Tibetan Buddhism.

Crossen sold his first story, "The Aaron Burr Murder Case," to *Detective Fiction Weekly* in September 1939, but says he didn't begin to make a living from writing till 1941. He tried his hand at publishing true crime magazines, comics, and a picture magazine, without great success, so he set out for Hollywood. From his typewriter flowed hundreds of stories, short novels for magazines, scripts radio, television, and film, nonfiction articles. He delved into science fiction in the 1950s, starting with "Restricted Clientele" (February 1951). His dystopian novels *Year of Consent* and *The Rest Must Die* also appeared in this decade.

In the course of his career Ken Crossen acquired six pseudonyms: Richard Foster, Bennett Barlay, Kent Richards, Clay Richards, Christopher Monig, and M.E. Chaber. The variety was necessary because different publishers wanted to reserve specific bylines for their own publications. Ken based "M.E. Chaber" on the Hebrew word for "author," *mechaber.*

In the early '50s, as M.E. Chaber, Crossen began to write a series of full-length mystery/espionage novels featuring Milo March, an insurance investigator. The first, *Hangman's Harvest,* was published in 1952. In all, there are twenty-two Milo March novels. One, *The Man Inside,* was made into a British film starring Jack Palance.

Most of Ken's characters were private detectives, and Milo was the most popular. Paperback Library reissued twenty-five Crossen titles in 1970–1971, with covers by Robert McGinnis. Twenty were Milo March novels, four featured an insurance investigator named Brian Brett, and one was about CIA agent Kim Locke.

Crossen excelled at producing well-plotted entertainment with fast-moving action. His research skills were a strong asset, back when research meant long hours searching library microfilms and poring over street maps and hotel floorplans. His imagination took him to many international hot spots, although he himself never traveled abroad. Like Milo March, he hated flying ("When you've seen one cloud, you've seen them all").

Ken Crossen was married four times. With his first wife he had three children (Stephen, Karen, Kendra) and with his second a son (David). He lived in New York, Florida, Southern California, Nevada, and other parts of the country. Milo March moves from Denver to New York City after five books of the series, with an apartment on Perry Street in Greenwich Village; that's where Ken lived, too. His and Milo's favorite watering hole was the Blue Mill Tavern, a short walk from the apartment.

Ken Crossen was a combination of many of the traits of his different male characters: tough, adventuresome, with a taste for gin and shapely women. But perhaps the best observation was made in an obituary written by sci-fi writer Avram Davidson, who described Ken as a fundamentally gentle person who had been buffeted by many winds.